IN DEFIANCE
OF DUTY

IN DEFIANCE OF DUTY

BY
CAITLIN CREWS

MILLS & BOON

First published in Great Britain 2011
by Mills & Boon, an imprint of Harlequin (UK) Limited.
Large Print edition 2012
Harlequin (UK) Limited, Eton House,
18-24 Paradise Road, Richmond, Surrey TW9 1SR

© Caitlin Crews 2012

ISBN: 978 0 263 23653 8

Harlequin (UK) policy is to use papers that are natural,
renewable and recyclable products and made from
wood grown in sustainable forests. The logging and
manufacturing process conform to the legal environmental
regulations of the country of origin.

Printed and bound in Great Britain
by CPI Antony Rowe, Chippenham, Wiltshire

To all the fantastic writers at the
2011 Romantic Writers of Australia Conference
who were so lovely and welcoming to me, despite
my crippling jetlag. It was such a treat (and an
honor) to get to spend time with you—
and I hope I did justice to your beautiful country!

And to my favorite Los Angeles–based Australian,
Kate Rogers, who told me the truth about magpies.

CHAPTER ONE

"LOVELY view."

Kiara didn't turn toward the deep, command-ing voice, even as it washed over her and some-how into her blood, her bones, making her very nearly shiver. She'd sensed his approach before he'd helped himself to the chair next to hers—there had been a certain expectant stillness in the air around her, a kind of palpable, electrically charged quiet, as if all of Sydney fell silent be-fore him. She'd pictured that easy, confident walk of his, the way his dark, powerful masculinity turned heads wherever he went, the way he'd no doubt been watching her with that intense, con-suming focus as he drew near.

But then, she'd been expecting him.

"That's a terrible pickup line," she pointed out, a shade too close to flippant. But she couldn't seem to help herself. She decided she wouldn't look at him unless he earned it. She would pretend to be enchanted by the water of the harbor, the coming sunset. Not by a man like him, no matter how tall, dark and dangerous he might be, even in her peripheral vision. "Especially here. This particular view is famous, I think you'll find. Renowned the world over."

"That should make it all the more lovely, then," he replied, a thread of amusement beneath the steel-and-velvet seduction of his voice. She felt it like heat, pressing into her skin. "Or are you the dreary sort who finds a view is spoiled forever if too many others look upon it?"

Kiara sat at a small outdoor table tucked in on the lower concourse beneath Sydney's glorious, soaring Opera House and the sky above, with full and unfettered access to the famous and beautiful arch of the Harbor Bridge opposite. The setting sun above had just settled into rich and tempting golds, sending the mellow light dancing over the sparkling water of the harbor itself, as if taunting the jutting skyscrapers of the city—as if daring them to look away from the spectacular evening show.

She certainly knew the feeling. And she wasn't even looking at the man who lounged next to her as if he owned the table, the chair, and her, too, though she was *aware* of him in every possible way. In every part of her skin and blood and bones.

"Don't try to change the subject," she said mildly, as if wholly unaffected by him and the great tractor beam of power and charisma that seemed to emanate from him. He was lethal. So compelling it almost hurt not to turn and let herself look at him, drink him in. "You're the one who trotted out a tired old line. I only pointed it out. I don't think that makes me dreary."

She knew intuitively that his particular brand of dark male beauty—so fierce and breathtaking, laced through with all that dizzying masculine power—would be equally dazzling if she dared turn her head and look at it. She could *feel* it. In the way her stomach clenched and, below, ached around a deep, feminine pulse. The way the fine hairs on her arms and the back of her neck stood at attention, almost making her shiver. The way the whole world seemed to shrink to just this table, this chair.

Him.

Instead, she fiddled with the coffee cup she'd

drunk dry a while ago, even toyed with the ends of the wavy light brown hair she'd swept back into a high ponytail, her hands betraying her even as she sat there with such studied carelessness, pretending she was unaware of the great strength of him next to her. The imposing fact of him— ink-black hair against oddly light eyes, the stamp of his Arab ancestry in his fierce features, and that mouthwatering fantasy of a body—that she could grasp even with only the briefest glance from the corner of her eye. The impact on not only her, but the whole of the Opera House Bar around them.

She could see the group of older women at the next table—the way they turned to look at him, then widened their eyes at each other before dissolving into besotted giggles better suited to the girls Kiara imagined they'd been some thirty years before.

"Tell me how to play this game," he said after a moment that seemed overripe with the gold sinking against the water, the murmur of the crowd of tourists all around them, his own dark magnetism spread over them like an umbrella. "Will I woo you with my wit? My appreciation of the local beauty? Perhaps I will tell you a series of pretty lies and convince you to come back to my hotel with me. Just for the night. Anonymous and furtive. Do you think that would work?"

"You won't know until you try," she said, biting back a grin, even as carnal images chased through her head—none of them either anonymous or furtive. All of them spellbinding. Wild with passion. "Though I hardly think laying out your options like that, so coldblooded and matter-of-fact, will do you any favors. You should think in terms of seduction, not spreadsheets." She found she was grinning despite herself then, but still kept from looking at him, staring resolutely ahead at the delicate arch of the bridge as if unable to tear herself away. "If you don't mind a word of advice."

"I relish it, of course." His low voice was cool, ironic, and still managed to kick up fires all along her skin. And deeper. She shifted in her seat, crossing and then recrossing her legs, wishing he did not take up *quite* so much space. He did not seem to move at all, and yet, somehow, she was even more aware of him.

"So far," she continued, her own voice confiding, pitched for his ears alone, "I must tell you that I'm completely unimpressed."

"With the view?" Now his amusement wasn't hidden at all. It moved through his voice even as it moved through her, teasing her with hints of something else beneath his crisp British public school vowels, something that indicated English was only one of his languages. The faintest suggestion that he was nothing simple or easily categorized. "I hope you're not one of those terminally bored socialite types, so shallow and endlessly fatigued by everything the world has to offer."

"And if I am?"

"That would be a great disappointment."

"Luckily," she said drily, "you can hardly have been too invested in something that could only have ended in lies and a furtive hotel visit, could you? I imagine the disappointment will be minor."

"But I am captivated," he protested in an insultingly mild way that made her laugh despite herself.

"By my profile?" She smiled at the bridge, imagined the man, and shook her head. "It's all you've seen of me."

"Perhaps it is your profile superimposed on such a famous view," he suggested. "I'm as awestruck as any run-of-the-mill tourist. If only I'd remembered my camera."

She forgot she didn't mean to look at him and turned her head.

It was looking into the sun. Searing. Dizzying.

He was beautiful—there was no other word for it—but there was nothing in the least bit pretty about him. He was a study in controlled ferocity. He was all sleek muscle and hard, strong lines. His rich black hair, his dark skin, the gleam in his unusual, near-blue eyes. The merciless thrust of his cheekbones, his belligerent jaw. He lounged beside her with seeming nonchalance, but she wasn't fooled.

He was all focus and menace, his rangy, athletic body showcased to perfection in a dark suit and a snow-white shirt that he wore open against his neck, as if he was attempting a casual gesture when everything else about him shouted out the formidable *force* he wore the way another man might wear a jacket. He looked as if there was nothing at all he couldn't do with his disconcertingly elegant hands—and nothing he hadn't already done with them. She could think of several possibilities, and had to swallow against the shocking surge of heat that swept through her then, wild and out of control.

She was sure he could feel the very same flames.

"Hello," he said quietly as their eyes met. Held. His sensual mouth curved into a knowing smile. "I like this view, too."

Kiara forced a jaded sigh. "You really aren't very good at this, are you?"

"Apparently not." His impossible eyes, somewhere between blue and green, or possibly gray, gleamed. "By all means, teach me. I live to serve."

She didn't laugh at that. She didn't need to. His own mouth quirked up in the corner, supremely arrogant and male, as if he was as unable to imagine himself serving anyone or anything as she was.

"For all you know, I could be meeting someone." She forgot about the view; he was far more mesmerizing, especially when his gaze turned darker and something like stormy. She smiled then. "My very jealous lover, for example, who might find you here and take out his aggression all over you. With his fists."

"A risk I feel prepared to take, somehow."

There was no denying the edge of confident menace in his smile then, and she wondered what sort of woman she was to find that as appealing as she did. Surely she ought to be ashamed. She wasn't.

"Is that a threat of violence?" she asked tartly. And then lied. "That's incredibly unattractive."

"That is exactly how you look," he said, the knowing quirk of his hard mouth deepening, his storm-tossed eyes too hot, too sure. "Un-attracted."

"Or perhaps I'm simply a single woman out on the town, looking for a date," she continued in the same nonchalant, careless tone. "You seem to want to talk only about the view. Or make depressing remarks about the *furtiveness* of a night of wild, uncontrollable passion. Neither is likely to make me want to date you, is it?"

"Are we talking about a date?" His mouth curved again, as if he was trying not to laugh, and very nearly failing. His almost-blue eyes reminded her of the winter sea, and were as compelling. "I thought this was a negotiation about sex. Endlessly inventive sex, I believe. Or hope, in any case. Not a tedious *date*, all manners and flowers and gentlemanlike behavior."

It took her a moment to breathe through the way he said *sex*, like some kind of incantation. Much less the images he conjured up, and their immediate effect on her body. How could one man be this dangerous? And why was she wholly unable to offer up any kind of defense against him?

"The way this works is that you pretend to be interested only in a date," she told him as if she was *this close* to exasperation but only the kindness of her heart kept her from it. "You *pretend* that you want to get to know me as a person. The more you do that, the more romantic it will all feel. To me, I mean. And that, of course, is the quickest route toward rampant sex in a hotel room." She shrugged her shoulders as if she felt she shouldn't have to be the one to share this with him. As if every other person in Sydney was well aware of this, and she wondered why he wasn't.

"I can't simply ask for rampant sex?" he asked, as if baffled. Possibly even shocked. Though that lazy, indulgent gleam in his eyes said otherwise. "Are you sure?"

"Only if you are planning to purchase it." She eyed him, and the hint of a smile that toyed with that mouth of his, and made her wish all sorts of undignified things. "Which is, of course, perfectly legal here. And no, buying me a drink is not the same thing."

"Your country has so many rules," he said softly, the amusement leaving his gaze as something far hotter took its place. "Mine is far more…direct."

She *felt* the way he looked at her, the fire in it moving over her like a caress, making her wish that she was dressed far more provocatively. Making her wish she could bare her skin to his gaze, to the night falling all around them. The black blazer she wore over a decadently soft black jumper and the dark blue jeans she'd tucked into her favorite black suede books felt confining, suddenly, instead of the casually chic look she'd been going for. She wished she could peel it all off and throw it all in the harbor. She wondered what it was about this man that made such an uncharacteristic urge seem so appealing in the first place.

But she knew.

"Direct?" she echoed, feeling the pull of that hard face, those unholy eyes. She wanted to move closer to that wicked mouth of his. She wanted it more than was wise. More than she should, out in public like this, where anyone could see. For a moment she forgot the game—*herself*—entirely.

"If I want it," he said quietly, so quietly, but she felt it flood into her as if he'd shouted it, as if he'd licked it into her skin, "I take it."

Kiara felt that hum in her, electric and something like overwhelming. For a moment she could only stare back at him, caught in that knowing gaze of his, as surely as if he'd caged her somehow. Trapped her as surely as if he'd used manacles and heavy iron bars. She shouldn't feel that like a thrill, twisting through her, but she did.

"Then I suppose I should count myself lucky that we are not in your country," she said after a moment, not sure until she spoke that she would be able to at all. She was surprised that her voice sounded so steady. Almost tart. "This is Australia. I'm afraid we're quite civilized."

"All of you in your new, young countries are the same," he said in that low tone, his voice its own dark spell, weaving its way over her, inside of her, as inexorable as the setting sun. "So brash, forever carrying on about your purported civility. But you are all so close, still, to your disreputable pasts, aren't you? All of it welling up from beneath, making a lie of these carefully cultivated facades."

Kiara realized two things simultaneously. One, that she could listen to him talk forever—about countries, about pasts, about whatever he liked. That voice of his triggered something deep inside her, something helpless and wanton, that made her breathless and so wrapped up in him that the world could fall to pieces around her and she wouldn't notice. Or, as now, the sun could disappear entirely beneath the horizon without her registering it, ushering in the inky sweetness of the Sydney night, and she would still see nothing but him.

And two, and more important, that she would die if she didn't touch him. Now.

"As fascinating as your thoughts on young countries and disreputable pasts may be," she said then, keeping her voice a low murmur, her eyes hot on his, "I think that I'd rather dispense with all this meaningless chatter and just get naked. What do you think?"

He smiled again, and she felt it shiver through her and curl her toes. He reached over and took her hand in his, carrying it to his mouth. It was the faintest hint of a kiss, a timeless gesture of chivalry for the benefit of the people all around them, but she felt it like a hard kick. Like a promise.

"There is nothing I would rather do," he said, that gleam of amusement in his eyes turning them something near silver. "But I'm afraid I'm meeting my wife for dinner. I'm sorry to disappoint you."

"I'm sure she'll understand." Kiara played with his strong fingers in hers. "Who would want to stand in the way of acrobatic, inventive sex, after all?"

"She's terribly jealous." He shook his head almost sadly. "It's like a sickness—*ouch*." His gaze turned baleful, and a silver heat gleamed there, while something almost too warm to bear echoed in a kind of sizzle low in Kiara's belly. "Did you just bite me?"

"Don't act like you didn't enjoy it." It was a dare.

He let go of her hand, but shifted closer, reaching over to pull gently on the end of her ponytail, tilting her head up slightly to meet his searing gaze.

"Perhaps I can risk my wife's jealous rages after all," he said musingly. He moved still closer, until their faces were a mere breath apart, his delectable mouth *just* there, *just* out of reach.

Her breath came out ragged, then, as if she'd broken into a run. She felt as if she had. His smile licked over her, into her.

"You look as if you can take it," Kiara agreed, and then she closed the distance between them and kissed him.

His wife, Sheikh Azrin bin Zayed Al Din, Crown Prince of Khatan, reflected with no little amusement, was endlessly delightful to him.

Her lips were soft and sweet against his, hinting at the passion that neither of them could succumb to out in the public eye like this. It was as frustrating as it was delicious. He wanted more than this *hint* of her, after two weeks apart. He wanted to taste her—take her—with a ferocity that might have surprised him, five years after marrying her, had he not been well used to this relentless thirst for her.

A thirst he could not indulge. Not here. Not now.

He pulled away, controlling himself with the ruthlessness that was second nature to him, particularly where his wife was concerned, and smiled again at the dazed look she wore, as if she had forgotten where they were. Azrin could look at her forever. Her pretty oval face with its delicate nose and brows, and her wide, decadent mouth that had been the first thing he'd noticed about her. Her hair was a mix of browns and golds, tumbling down past her shoulders in light waves unless, like tonight, she'd opted to put the heavy weight of it up in one of her sleek, deceptively casual styles. She looked taller than she was, her body firm and toned from her years of athletics and hard work, and she tended to dress conservatively as suited her position, yet with a quiet little flair that was hers alone.

That deep current of wickedness was all for him.

"If you had spoken to me like that when we met," he said lazily, taunting her, "I doubt I would ever have pursued you at all. So disrespectful and challenging."

She rolled her eyes, as he'd known she would. "I did speak to you like that," she replied. Her generous mouth widened into a smile. "You loved it."

"So I did."

He got to his feet then and took her hand to help her rise. She held on for a moment too long, as if she wanted to cling to even that much contact. He felt the kick of it, of her, deep inside of him. He craved her. He wanted to lick his way over every inch of her skin, relearning her as if the two weeks he'd been without her might have changed her. He wanted to find out for himself. With his mouth, his hands.

She curved into his side as they began to walk back along the concourse toward Sydney's impressive, glittering array of skyscrapers, and the penthouse he kept there that was as much a primary residence as anything could be for two people who traveled as much as they did. He slid his arm around her slender shoulders and contented himself as best he could with a light kiss on the top of her head that barely reached his chin. Her hair smelled of sunshine and flowers, and he could not touch her the way he wanted to.

Not here. Not now. *Not yet*, he thought.

No unrestrained public displays of affection for the Crown Prince of Khatan and his non-Khatanian, scandalous-merely-by-virtue-of-her-foreign-birth princess. Well did Azrin know the rules. The public—particularly in his country—might fight for any possible glimpse of what they called his *modern Cinderella romance*, but that didn't mean they wanted to see anything that wouldn't have suited the family-friendly film of the same name.

There could be nothing that suggested that Azrin was compromised in any way by what many in his country took to be the lax moral code of anyone not from their own part of the world. There could certainly be no hint that the passion between Azrin and his princess was still so intense, so all-encompassing, that some days they did not even get out of bed, even after all this time. He was hoping that this night might lead directly into one of those lost days, even though he knew there was so much to do now, so many details to take care of and so little time to do it all in…

He should tell her now. Immediately. He knew that he should—that there was no real excuse for waiting. There was only his curious inability to speak up as he should. There was only that part of him that didn't want to accept this was happening.

He wanted this one night, that was all. This last, perfect night of the life they'd both enjoyed so much for so long that had let him pretend he was someone else. What was one night more?

"I missed you, Azrin," Kiara whispered, her supple body flush against his, her arm around his waist as they walked. "Two weeks is much too long."

"It was unavoidable." He heard the dark note in his voice and smiled down at her to dispel it. "I didn't care for it, either."

He would be happy when this part of their life was behind them, he thought as they made their way through the usual crowds flocking to Sydney's pretty jewel of a harbor to enjoy the mild evening, the restaurants, the view. He would be more than pleased to do without these weeks of separations that they tried valiantly to keep to ten days or less. The endless grind of international travel to this or that city, in every corner of the globe, to steal a day, a night, even an afternoon together. Meeting up with his wife in hotels that became interchangeable in the cities where they did not have a residence, and hardly noticing which residence was which when they were in one of them. New York, Singapore, Tokyo, Paris, the capital city of his own country, Arjat an-Nahr, on an endlessly repeating cycle. Always having to plan to see his wife around the demands of their calendars, never simply seeing her. Never really able to simply *be* with her.

He would not miss this part of their life at all. He told himself that having this part end would be worth the rest of it. At least they would be together. Surely that was the important thing.

"You should not have stayed so long in Arjat an-Nahr," she was saying, that teasing note in her voice, the one that normally made him smile automatically. "I'm tempted to think that you care more for your country and its demands on your time than your poor, neglected wife."

He knew she was kidding. Of course she was. But still—tonight, it pricked at him. It seemed to suggest things about their future that he knew he didn't want to hear. That he could not accept, not even as an offhanded joke. It cut too deep tonight.

"I will be king one day," he reminded her, keeping his voice light, because he knew—he did—that she was only teasing, the way she often did. The way she always had. Wasn't her very irreverence why he had been so drawn to her in the first place? "Everything will come second to my country then, Kiara. Even you."

And him, of course. Especially him.

She looked up at him, those marvelous brown eyes of hers moving over his face in the dark. He knew that she could read him, and wondered what she saw. Not the truth, of course. He knew even she could not know that, not from a single searching look, no matter how well she could read what she saw. No one knew the truth yet save his father's doctors, his mother and Azrin himself.

"I know who I married," she told him softly, though Azrin did not think she could when he felt so unsure of it himself. "Do you doubt it?" She smiled; soothing, somehow, what felt so raw in him that easily. As if she could sense it without his having to tell her. And then her voice took on that teasing lilt again, encouraging him to follow her back into lighter, shallower waters. "You always take such pains to remind me, after all."

It was only change, he told himself. Everything changed. Even them. Even this. It was neither good nor bad—it was simply the natural order of things.

And more than that, he had always known this day was coming. Why had he imagined otherwise, these past five years? Who had he been trying to fool?

"Do you mean when I request that you keep your voice down while you are pretending that I am merely some overconfident stranger picking you up in a bar, lest the papers feel the need to share this game of yours with the whole world?" He couldn't quite make his voice sound reproving, especially not when her brown eyes were so warm, so challenging, and seemed to connect directly with his sex. And his heart. "Does that count as taking pains, Kiara? Or is it simply a more highly developed sense of self-preservation?"

"Yes, my liege," she murmured in feigned obeisance, laughter thrumming in her voice, just below the surface. She even bowed her head in a mock sign of respect. "Whatever you say, my liege."

His almost equally feigned look of exasperation made her laugh, and the bright, musical sound of it seemed to roll through him like light.

He couldn't regret the past five years. He didn't.

He had always taken his duties as Crown Prince as seriously as he'd taken his position as the managing director of the Khatan Investment Authority, one of the largest sovereign wealth funds in the world. Kiara had always been wholly dedicated to her own role as vice president of her family's famous winery in South Australia's renowned Barossa Valley, a career that took her all over the world and kept her as busy as he was. Theirs had always been a modern marriage, the only one like it in the whole of his family's history.

But then, he had long been his country's emblem of the future, whether he wanted to be or not—and no one had ever asked him his feelings on the subject. His feelings were irrelevant, Azrin knew. While his father was very much and very proudly wedded to the old ways, Azrin was supposed to represent the modern age come to life in the midst of old-world Khatan, his small, oil-rich island nation in the Persian Gulf.

He knew—had always known—that once he took the throne he was expected to usher in the new era of Khatan that his father either could not or did not want to. He was expected to lead his people into a freer, more independent future, without the bloodshed and turmoil some of their neighboring countries had experienced.

And Kiara had been his first step in that direction, little as he might have thought of her in those terms when he'd met her. She was a twenty-first century Western woman in every respect, independent and ambitious, a fourth generation Australian winemaker and wholly impressive in her own right. Marrying her had been a commitment to a very different kind of future than the one his old school father, with his traditional three wives, offered their people.

Together, Azrin and Kiara were considered the new face of a new Khatan. That wouldn't change now—it would only become more analyzed and critiqued. More speculated about. More observed and remarked upon. Their marriage would cease to be theirs; it would become his people's, just as the rest of his life would. It was inevitable.

Azrin had always known this day would come. He just hadn't expected it would come *now*. So soon. And perhaps because he'd thought he would have so many more years left before it happened, he certainly hadn't understood until now how very much he'd dreaded it.

He didn't want to admit that, not even to himself.

"Where have you gone?" she asked now, stopping, and thereby making him stop, too. The busy Sydney Pier bristled with ferries and commuters headed home for the evening, tourist groups and restaurant patrons on their way to an evening out. Her clever eyes met his as her palm curved against his jaw. "You're miles away."

"I am still in Khatan," he said, which was true

enough. He took her hand in his, lacing their fingers together, and tugged her along with him as he started to walk again, guiding her around the usual cluster of stalls and street performers making the most of the evening rush and the ever-present tourists. "But I would much rather be in you. Naked, I think you said?"

"I did say that." Her voice was so proper, so demure. Only because he knew her well could he hear the mischief beneath the surface, that touch of wickedness that made him harden in response. "I thought you might have forgotten. My liege."

"I never forget anything that has to do with your naked body, Kiara," he said in a low voice. "Believe me."

He wasn't ready, he thought—and yet he must be. What he wanted, what he felt—none of that mattered any longer. What mattered was who he was, and therefore who he was about to become. He simply had to learn to keep his own desires, his own feelings, in reserve, just as he'd done for years before he'd met Kiara. In truth, it had been nothing but selfishness that had allowed him to spend the past five years pretending it could ever be otherwise.

He handed Kiara into the long black car that idled at the curb once they reached the street and climbed in after her.

Despite the fact that they were a prince and a princess, a royal sheikh and his chosen bride, they had spent years behaving as if they were like any other high-powered couple anywhere else in the world. They'd believed it themselves, Azrin thought. He certainly had.

The Prince and Princess of Khatan were relatable, accessible. *Normal.* They worked hard and didn't get to see as much of each other as they'd like. Theirs was not a story of harems and exoticism, royal excesses and the bizarre lifestyles of the absurdly privileged. They were your everyday, run-of-the-mill power couple, just trying to excel at what they did. *Just like you.*

And yet they were not those couples, and never would be.

They were not normal. They had only been pretending. He told himself it was not a kind of grief that gripped him then—that it was simply reality.

He would be king. She would be his queen. There were greater expectations of those roles than of the ones they'd been playing at all this time. There were different, more complicated considerations. He knew with the kick of something like foreboding, deep in his gut, that there were great sacrifices that both of them would have to make.

It was only change, he told himself again. Everything and everyone changed.

But not tonight.

CHAPTER TWO

IT TOOK Kiara long moments after she woke in the wide, plush bed in the center of a room bathed in light to recall that she was in Sydney. In the penthouse in Sydney, she reminded herself as she stretched—that glorious multi-level dwelling high on the top of an exclusive building that only Azrin, who had been raised between several palaces, could call *an apartment*. Her lips curved.

She swung her legs over the side of the platform bed and rose slowly, smiling at the delicious feeling of bonelessness all throughout her body. That was the Azrin effect. She supposed she should have been used to it by now. Images of the previous night swept through her head, each more erotic than the last. He was a sensualist, her husband; a demanding lover who held nothing back—and took everything in return.

She found herself in the opulent shower with no real idea how she'd got there, humming to herself as she used the delicately scented soap over the skin he'd tasted and touched repeatedly. That was what he did—he made her a besotted, airheaded fool. When he was near, she found she could think of very little else.

Just him. Only him.

She stepped from the great glass shower that she knew from past experience could hold both of them as well as some of Azrin's more inventive fantasies, and toweled herself off, letting her hair down from the clip she'd used to secure it away from the hot spray. Sometimes she felt guilty that she often considered her demanding career a necessary a bit of breathing room between rounds with her far more demanding, far more consuming husband. There was just something about Azrin, she thought, smiling to herself, that encouraged complete surrender.

She found him out in the great room, lounging carelessly on the low sofa that sprawled out in the center of the sleek, modern space, speaking in assured and confident Arabic into the tablet he used for video conferencing. His fierce gaze met hers and though he did not smile, a flash of heat moved through her anyway.

Even after the night they'd shared, she wanted more. Her core warmed anew, ready for him at a glance. Again. Always.

He was lethal.

She made sure to keep out of sight of the camera, slipping into the open-plan gourmet kitchen that neither she nor Azrin had ever cooked in to fix herself a morning coffee from the imposing, gleaming espresso machine. A few minutes later she settled with the fruits of her labor—a flat white in a warm ceramic mug, perfectly made if she said so herself—on one of the chrome bar stools that fetched up to the shiny granite expanse of kitchen counter.

She still did not speak Arabic, though she'd picked up a few phrases over the years, none of them particularly repeatable outside of the bedroom. So she didn't try to figure out what he was talking about in that commanding tone that reminded her that he was a royal prince who some called *my liege* without irony; she let his deep, sure voice wash over her like a caress. She sat and enjoyed a rare moment with nothing to do but look out the wall of floor-to-ceiling glass windows that faced north, the spectacular view stretching across the green lushness of Hyde Park toward the gorgeous Royal Botanic Gardens, the soaring shapes of the Sydney Opera House, and the picturesque Sydney Harbor, all of it bathed in the sweet, golden Australian sunshine.

But she couldn't keep it up. Too soon she was worrying over a problem that had cropped up with the export of one of the Zinfandels they'd been experimenting with in recent years, and wondering if it required a quick, unscheduled call to her mother, the formidable CEO of Frederick Wines and sometime bane of Kiara's existence. Given the complicated cocktail of guilt, love and obligation that characterized Kiara's relationship with her mother as both her daughter and her second-in-command, Kiara usually preferred to handle things like this on her own. She argued the pros and cons in her head, going back and forth again and again.

Sydney preened before her in the abundant sunshine, skyscrapers sparkling in the light and the harbor dotted with sails and ferry boats far below, but Kiara hardly saw them. In her mind, she saw the greens and golds of her beloved Barossa Valley, the rich green vineyards spreading out in all directions, the complacent little towns bristling with Bavarian architecture, built by settlers like Kiara's ancestors who'd fled from religious persecution in Prussia. She saw the family vineyards that had dominated her life since she was a girl—and the grand old chateau that had been in her family for generations.

The winery had taken over her mother's life when she'd found herself there, a widow with an infant, and it was Kiara's life, too, as it could hardly be anything else. At the very least, she had to prove to both her mother and herself that it had all been worth it, didn't she? All the years of sacrifice and struggle on her mother's part to build and maintain Kiara's heritage—surely Kiara owed her, at the very least, her own commitment to that heritage.

She wasn't sure what made her look up to find Azrin watching her then, his conference clearly over and an unusually serious look on his ruthless face.

"Good morning," she said and smiled, pushing her concerns away as she drank him in, as if he could clear her head and vanquish her mother's doubt just by being there in front of her. Instead of halfway across the world somewhere, available only by phone or video chat, which was the way she usually saw him.

She expected him to smile back. But he only looked at her for a long moment, and something twisted inside her—something she didn't entirely understand. She remembered, then, his unusual urgency the night before. The edge to him that had made him even more fierce, even more demanding than usual. Something skittered down her spine, making her sit straighter on the stool. She smoothed the edges of her silk wrapper around her. She didn't look away.

"Why are you looking at me like that?" she asked softly. "What's happened?"

"I am admiring my beautiful wife," he said, though there was a certain rawness in his near-blue eyes. "My princess. My future queen."

Kiara was uneasy, and she didn't know why. He looked as if he'd been up for hours, which was not particularly remarkable, given his many business concerns and the world's various time zones. His dark hair looked rumpled, as if he'd been running his hands through it repeatedly. He hadn't bothered to shave, and the rough shadow along his tough jaw made him look more like the sheikh she sometimes forgot he was and less like the cosmopolitan, sophisticated husband with whom she explored the great modern cities of the world.

For some reason, her throat was dry.

"You could sound a *bit* less complimentary," she pointed out, trying to sound as teasing and as light as she usually did. "If you tried. Though you'd have to work hard at it."

He nearly smiled then, and she had the strange notion that it was against his will. Something sat heavy in the room, making her anxious, and she could see he felt it, too—that it was in him, something grim and hard behind his gaze, making those near-blue eyes grow dark. Making it difficult to breathe.

Kiara prided herself on her ability to close deals and navigate the sometimes treacherous labyrinth of international business concerns in general and the wine industry in particular. Hell, she was good at it. She'd had to be, having had to overcome the usual suspicions that she'd been promoted thanks to her relationship with the boss lady rather than her own hard work, and then, after her wedding, having to stare down everyone who'd sniggered and snidely called her *your highness* or *princess* in the middle of a tense meeting.

She enjoyed confounding expectations, thank you very much. She'd learned how to keep people at arm's length as a defense mechanism against her mother's complete lack of boundaries when she was still a girl. She'd spent her professional life cultivating a little bit of an untouchable ice-queen facade, and becoming a widely photographed and speculated-about princess had only helped make her deliberate shell that much more impenetrable. She liked it that way.

But *this* man was different. *This* man looked at her with some kind of pain in him and she would do anything—dance, tease, crawl, whatever worked—to make it go away. This was Azrin, and the love she felt for him—the love that had crashed into her and wholly altered the course of her life five years ago—was impossible to hide away behind some smooth mask. He was the one person on earth that she never, ever wanted at arm's length, no matter how wild and unbalanced that sometimes made her feel inside, and no matter how far away from each other they often were.

She was up and on her feet before she knew she meant to move, crossing over to him.

"I have something to tell you," he said, his gaze still so dark, so bleak.

"Then tell me," she said. But she straddled him where he sat, letting her silk wrapper fall open to show that she was naked and still warm from her shower beneath it. "But you'll forgive me if I make the conversation a little more exciting, won't you?"

She wasn't really thinking. She only knew she wanted to soothe him, and to *do* something to make whatever this was better. She felt him harden beneath her, felt his breath against her neck, as if he was as helpless to resist this pull between them as she had always been.

But she knew they both were. It had been this way, outsized and impossible and wholly irresistible, from the very beginning.

"Kiara…" he said, in that tone that was supposed to be reproving, chastising even, but his hands slid beneath the wrapper and onto her bare skin, smoothing over her hips. She arched against him, feeling the scrape of his jaw against the tender slope of her breast. He tilted his head back to look up at her, his hard mouth in an unsmiling line. "What are you doing?"

She thought that was obvious, but she only smiled, and rolled her hips, the heat and strength of him against the softest part of her. She ached as if she'd never had him. She burned as if he was already deep within her. And his eyes lit with that same fire, and she knew he felt it, too.

Holding his gaze, she reached down between them and released him from his trousers with impatient hands, stroking his silken length, driving herself a little bit wild. Still watching him, those unholy eyes and his fierce, uncompromising face, she shifted up and over him, then sank down, sheathing him hard and deep within her.

"I'm distracting you," she told him, her voice uneven.

"Or possibly killing me," he muttered, taking her mouth with his in a long, hard kiss. "As I suspect is your plan."

She moved against him, rocking him deeper into her, unable to bite back her own small sigh of pleasure. He moved with her until she started to shake, and then he took control. His hands gripped her hips, preventing her from rocking against him when she wanted to tip herself over the edge.

"What are you doing?" she demanded, her voice a mere scrap of ragged sound, and his smile made her shiver.

"Distracting you," he said, his cool eyes glittering with that sensual promise that made her feel nearly giddy. "You'll come when I tell you to, Kiara, and not before."

She wanted to argue, but he moved then, and she could do nothing at all but move with him, surrendering to his hands, his wicked mouth, and his dark, whispered commands. Letting him build the fire between them into an out of control blaze. Letting him take them both exactly where she wanted to go.

And when he finally ordered her to come, she did, screaming out his name.

Azrin could not understand why he didn't simply tell her.

Why he hadn't told her already. Why some part of him didn't want to tell her at all.

They'd had the one last, long night. Drawing it out any further was nothing more than the very kind of selfishness he could no longer allow himself.

She was still in the shower. He could see the shape of her through the steamy glass, and he already regretted having left the warm embrace of the hot water. He could have stayed in there with her, and continued this exercise in pretense, in misdirection, as if they could lose themselves enough in each other that the whole world would go away.

Perhaps that was what he wanted. If he was honest, he knew that it was.

Hadn't that been what Kiara had always been for him? A step away from the expected—an escape from the traditional?

Enjoy yourself while you can, his father had said when he'd married, his creased face canny, knowing. As unsympathetic as ever, the old man as harsh a ruler of his family as he was of his country. *You will pay for it all soon enough, I promise you.*

Because his father had known, too: Kiara was Azrin's way of asserting himself in a life that would too soon be swallowed whole by duty and sacrifice. There would be no escape.

But Kiara had been his. All his. He'd been unable to resist her. She was his most selfish act of all, having nothing whatsoever to do with the things that were expected of him, the things he expected of himself. He had been meant to marry a woman like his own mother—one of the exquisite Khatanian girls who had been trotted out before him at every social opportunity since he was a boy, each more perfect than the last, each competing to show herself to be the most obvious choice for Azrin's future queen.

They were indistinguishably attractive, impeccably mannered and becomingly modest. They were all from powerful, noble families, all raised with the same set of ideals and expectations, all bred to be perfect wives and excellent mothers, all taught from birth to anticipate and tend to a man's every passing whim—and if that man was to be their king? All the better.

Instead, he'd met Kiara in a crowded little laneway in Melbourne. He had been walking off his jet lag as he prepared for a week's worth of meetings with some of the city's financial leaders.

He'd ducked into one of the narrow alleys that snaked behind a typical Melbourne street featuring a jumble of sleek modern skyscrapers and Victorian-era facades, and had found his way to a tiny café that had reminded him of one of his favorite spots in Paris. His bodyguard had cleared the way for him to claim a seat at one of the tiny tables overlooking the busy little lane—perhaps a touch overzealously.

"I think you'll find it's customary to *pretend* to apologize when stealing a table from someone else," she had said, a teasing note in her voice that made her sound as if she was about to bubble over into laughter. As if there was something impossibly merry, very nearly golden, inside her just bursting to come out. That had been his first impression of Kiara—that voice.

Then he'd looked up. He'd never been able to account for the way that first look at her, when she'd been a stranger and speaking to him as if she found him both unimpressive in the extreme *and* somewhat ridiculous—not something that had ever happened to him before—had struck him like that. Like an unerring blow straight to the solar plexus.

First he'd seen that mouth. It had hit him. Hard. He'd seen her brown eyes, much too intelligent and direct, with the same arch look in them that he'd heard in her voice. He'd had the impression of her pretty face, her hair thrown back into a careless twist at the back of her head. It had been winter in Melbourne, and she'd dressed for it in boots and tights beneath some kind of flirty little skirt, and a sleek sort of coat with a bright red scarf wrapped about her neck. She had been all edges and color, attitude and mockery, and should not have attracted or interested him in any possible way.

"But as you and your entourage are fairly bristling with self-importance," she'd continued in that same tone, waving a hand at his bodyguard and himself with an obvious lack of the respect he'd usually received, which Azrin had found entirely too intriguing in spite of himself, "I can only assume that you see café tables as one more thing you are compelled to conquer." She'd smiled, which had not detracted from her sarcasm in any way. "In which case, have at. You clearly need it more than I do."

She'd turned to go, and Azrin had found that

unbearable. He hadn't allowed himself to question why that should be, or, worse, why he should feel compelled to act on that unprecedented feeling.

"Please," he'd said, shocking his usually un-flappable bodyguard almost as much as he'd shocked himself—as Azrin was not known for his interest in sharp-mouthed, clever-eyed girls who took too much pleasure in public dressing-downs. "Join me. You can enumerate my many character flaws, and I will buy you a coffee for your troubles."

She'd turned back to him, a considering sort of light in her captivating eyes, and a smile moving across that generous mouth of hers.

"I can do that alone," she'd pointed out, her smile deepening. "I'm already doing it in my head, as a matter of fact."

"Think of how much more satisfying it will be to abuse me to my face," he'd said silkily. "How can you resist that kind of challenge?"

As it turned out, she couldn't.

Azrin had spent the rest of the afternoon try-ing to convince her to join him for dinner at his hotel, and the rest of his time in Melbourne try-ing to persuade her to go to bed with him. He'd managed only the dinner that night and then a week of the same, and he was not a man who had before then had even a passing acquaintance with failure of any sort.

He hadn't known how to process it. He'd told himself that had been why he'd been so unreasonably obsessed with this woman who had treated him so cavalierly, who had laughed at him when he'd tried to seduce her, and yet whose kisses had nearly taken off the back of his head when she'd condescended to bestow them upon him.

"You want the chase, not me," she'd informed him primly on his last night in Melbourne.

She had just stopped another kiss from going too far, and had even removed herself from Azrin's grasp, stepping back against the wall outside the door to her flat, into which she'd steadfastly refused to invite him. Again.

He'd had the frustrating suspicion that she was about to leave him standing there.

Again.

"What if I want *you*?" he'd asked, that wholly unfamiliar frustration bleeding into his voice and tangling in the air between them. "What if the chase is nothing but an impediment?"

"What a delightful fantasy," she'd replied—
though he already knew that was not quite true,
that careless tone she adopted. "But I'm afraid
that your great, romantic pursuit of me will have
to take a backseat to my graduate studies. I'm
sure you understand. Dark and brooding princes
tend to turn out to be little more than fairy-tale
interludes, in my experience—"

"You have vast experience with princes, do
you?" His tone had been sardonic, but she'd ignored him anyway.

"—while I really do require my Masters in
Wine Technology and Viticulture to get on with
my real life." She'd smiled at him, even as he'd
registered the way she'd emphasized the word
real. "I'll understand if you want to throw a little
bit of a strop and sulk all the way back to your
throne. No one will think any the less of you."

"Kiara," he'd said then, unable to keep his
hands off her, and wanting more than just the
simple pleasure of his palm over the curve of
her upper arm, which was what he'd had to settle
for. She was not for him—he'd known that—but
he'd been completely incapable of accepting it
as he should. "Prepare yourself for the fairy-tale

interlude. I may have to go to Khatan tomorrow morning, but I'll be back."

"Of course you will," she'd said, smiling as if she'd known better.

But he'd come back, as promised. Again and again. Until she'd finally started to believe him.

He watched her now, his unexpected princess, as she climbed from the shower and wrapped herself in one of the soft towels. She smiled at him, and he felt something clench inside of him. She had never wanted to be a queen. She hadn't even wanted to be a princess. She'd wanted him, that was all, just as he'd wanted her. Perhaps it had been foolish to imagine that that kind of connection, that impossible need, could be enough.

But foolish or not, this was the bed they'd made.

And now it was time to lie in it, whether he liked it or not. Whether *she* liked it or not.

Whether he wanted to be the King of Khatan or not—which had never mattered before, he reminded himself sharply, and certainly didn't matter now. It simply *was*.

"My father's cancer is back," he said abruptly.

* * *

"Azrin, no," Kiara breathed, as she tried to process his words.

He did not move from his position in the doorway. He leaned against the doorjamb with seeming nonchalance, beautiful and yet somehow remote, in nothing but dark trousers he hadn't bothered to fully button. But she could see the grim lines around his mouth, and the tension gripping his long frame. And the dark gray of his eyes, focused on her in a way that she could not quite understand.

"He plans to fight it, of course," he said in that same, oddly detached way, as if he was forcing himself to get through this by rote. As if this was the preview to something much bigger. Something worse. What that might be, Kiara did not want to imagine. "He is nothing if not ornery."

"I'm so sorry," Kiara said, her head spinning. It was difficult to imagine the old king, Azrin's belligerent and autocratic father, anything but his demanding and robust self. It was impossible to imagine that even cancer would dare try to beat King Zayed, when nothing and no one else had ever come close to loosening the iron grip he held on his country, his throne. His only son.

"He does not seem particularly concerned that it will kill him this time," Azrin continued. He shifted then, thrusting his hands into the pockets of his trousers. His mouth twisted. "But then, he has always had an exalted sense of himself. It is what led to the worst excesses of his reign. He leaves the wailing and gnashing of teeth to my mother."

Queen Madihah was the first of the old king's three wives. That and her production of the Crown Prince rendered her a national treasure. She was the very model of serene, gracious, modestly restrained Khatanian femininity, and as such, had always made Kiara feel distinctly brash and unpolished by comparison. It was impossible to imagine her changing expression, much less wailing.

"He's in excellent health otherwise," she said, thinking of the last time she'd seen her father-in-law, sometime the previous spring. He had insisted she join him for a long walk in the palace gardens, and despite the fact that Kiara regularly put in time on treadmills in gyms all over the world, the pace the older man had set had left her close to winded. That and the way he'd interrogated her, as if he was still suspicious of her relationship with his son and heir, as if he expected her to reveal her true motives at any moment, whatever those might be. "You would never know he was in his seventies…"

Something moved across Azrin's face then, and she let the words trail away.

"He has announced that he is an old man, and has only the weapons to fight one battle left in him," he said. Kiara felt frozen in place, and she didn't understand it. It was something to do with the way he was looking at her, the set to his jaw, that made her…nervous. Much too nervous. "He doesn't think he can care for the kingdom and for himself, not now. Not the way he did the last time."

"Whatever he needs to do to beat it," Kiara said immediately. Staunchly. "And whatever we need to do to help him."

The silence seemed to stretch taut between them.

"He is stepping aside, Kiara," Azrin said. Almost gently, yet with that steel beneath that made a kind of panic curl into something thick and hot in her belly. "Retiring."

For a moment, she didn't know what he meant.

"Of course," she said, when his meaning penetrated. "It will be good practice for you to take the throne while he recovers, won't it?"

"No." Again, that voice. His eyes so hard on hers. As if she was letting him down—had already done so—and she didn't know how that could have happened without her knowing it. Without her meaning to do it. She locked her knees beneath her, afraid, suddenly, that they might tremble and betray the full scope of her agitation.

"No?" she echoed. "It won't be good practice?"

"It won't be temporary. He is stepping aside for good."

She blinked. He waited. Something inside her seemed to go terribly still. As if she could not comprehend what he was telling her. But she did.

"That means—" She stopped herself. She had the urge to laugh then, but knew, somehow, that she did not dare. That he would not forgive her if she did, not now. She shook her head.

"It means I will be the new king of Khatan in

six short weeks," Azrin said in that strong, sure voice, as if that hardness was a part of him now, as if it was part of who he was becoming. As if it was a necessary precursor to the throne.

"Six weeks?" Kiara did laugh then, slightly. Her voice seemed too high, too uncertain. "I'd hardly got used to you being a prince over five years of marriage. I can't get my head around you being *king* in a little more than a month!"

She thought he might smile at that, but his mouth remained that flat, stern line. His eyes were the coldest she'd ever seen them. She felt, again, as if she'd been thrown neck deep into something that she ought to understand, but didn't.

"You don't have to get your head around it," he said with a kind of distant formality that made her tense up in response. "I've been getting my head around becoming king my whole life. This was always going to happen—it's just happening a bit more quickly than I'd originally anticipated."

Pull yourself together, Kiara ordered herself then, suddenly aware that she was standing stock still in the middle of the bathroom floor, staring at him as if he'd transformed into some kind of monster before her very eyes. Hardly the way a good, supportive spouse should behave at such a time.

She imagined there was no one in the world who wouldn't feel out of their depth at a moment like this. Thrones! Kings! But this was her husband. This was real. She could sort out her own feelings later. *In private.* She walked over to him, rising on her toes to press a kiss against his hard jaw.

"This can't be easy," she said softly. "But I love you. We'll figure it out."

"I suspect he must be sicker than he wishes to let on," Azrin said, his voice gruff. "He always promised he would die before he abdicated." He let out a sound that was not quite a laugh. "But then, he took the throne when he was all of nineteen. There was only one way to hold it. He came by his ruthlessness honestly."

She kissed him again, determined to ignore that tension simmering in him and all around them. She knew that Azrin's relationship with his father had never been easy. That the king had never been pleased with the way the kingdom viewed Azrin as some kind of savior-in-waiting.

Azrin had always said that if his father had only managed to have another son, Azrin would never have remained his heir. But he hadn't.

This is real, she told herself again.

"You can do this," she said. "You've been preparing for years. You're ready."

"Yes, Kiara. I'm ready," he said quietly, his eyes again too dark, his mouth too grim.

Something gripped her then, some kind of terror, but she shoved it aside, annoyed with herself. Again. Was she really so self-involved? She could only stare up at him as he ran a hand over the back of her head, smoothing down her wet hair, gently tipping her head back to gaze at him more fully.

Azrin's mouth curved slightly then, though it was in no way a smile, the way she wanted it to be. His gaze seared into hers, and she was afraid, suddenly, of the things he might see there.

"But are you?" he asked.

CHAPTER THREE

IT WAS a question her own mother echoed a week later when Kiara was back at the winery, trying to handle her responsibilities in one part of her life so she could go to Khatan and do her duty in the other part.

She'd assured Azrin she was ready and willing to do it. Eager, even. She'd been so earnest she'd nearly convinced herself.

Nearly.

"Are you honestly prepared to be a *queen*, Kiara?" her mother asked coolly, as if she'd looked inside and managed to articulate all the dark and unpleasant things Kiara was pretending she didn't feel. "This isn't a game, you know. Khatan's monarchy is not ornamental."

Kiara forced herself to silently count to ten, sitting there in her mother's pretty office with the breathtaking view out across the Frederick vineyards, green and healthy-looking in the afternoon light—not that she could concentrate on that now, though the view usually calmed her down. She had to keep herself from succumbing to the temper she knew her mother would view as a weakness. And, worse, as a confirmation.

Besides, she was all too aware that the temper was just a camouflage for the guilt that lay beneath. A lifetime of guilt, because she knew she was the reason her mother had dedicated her life to this place, these vineyards, after Kiara's father had died. Without Kiara, who knew what Diana might have done with her life?

Was it any wonder that Kiara was in no rush to have any babies herself?

One, two, three...

She eyed her mother across the wide expanse of Diana's always-neat desk, seeing far too much of herself in the older woman. As ever. It was like looking into some version of her future, much as she preferred to deny it to herself. The same narrow shoulders and long-legged frame. The same way of holding themselves, though Kiara knew she would never have her mother's innate elegance. That was all Diana.

Kiara was the only one who had seen beneath

her mother's polished exterior. She was the only one who knew what it had cost Diana to give up so much for this place. For Kiara. For the legacy she thought Kiara's father would have wanted to give her himself, if he could have done.

Five, six, seven...

Diana had taken over the Frederick wine business with more determination than skill after her husband's early death, and had ushered it into its current state of prominence by the force of her will alone. She'd hardly been around at all during Kiara's formative years, leaving the day to day raising of her daughter to Kiara's late grandmother, Diana's mother-in-law. And yet none of that prevented Diana from being far too opinionated about the choices she thought Kiara should have made. And judgmental about the ones Kiara actually had made.

Meaning, her mother did not approve of Azrin. At all. Of what he *represented*, as she liked to put it. She thought that Kiara should have married that nice Harry Thompson who'd been her first boyfriend, whose family was also deeply entrenched in the Barossa Valley—and who could, she had always maintained, *understand* Kiara in a way Azrin never would.

And somewhere deep inside, where guilt and obligation mixed into something sharp-edged and prickly, a part of Kiara had always wondered if Diana was right. She wondered it even more today, as she prepared for a role she and Azrin had never discussed in any detail, both assuming it was too far off in the future to bother worrying about.

Was she prepared to be his queen?

She couldn't forgive Diana for asking the question she didn't dare ask herself.

Eight, nine...

"Why wouldn't I be prepared, Mother?" she asked, aware that her voice was more strained than it should have been, clearly indicating that the question had got under her skin. She felt as if she'd lost points before she'd started—an all-too familiar feeling where her mother was concerned. She willed herself to exude the kind of cool poise that she was known for everywhere else but here. "I knew who Azrin was when I married him."

She'd known who he was the moment she'd

laid eyes on him. Too powerful. Too dangerous. Too overwhelming and much too ruthless. She might have fallen in love with him, but that didn't change the basic facts about who he was. She'd never lost sight of that. Had she?

"When you married him he was a financier who happened to be a prince, and he was perfectly happy to traipse about the globe with you," Diana said in that seemingly nonchalant way of hers that immediately put Kiara's back up. Nothing about Diana was nonchalant. Not ever. "Now he will be a king, which is not the same thing at all, is it?"

"He was always going to be a king." Kiara's voice was much too cross, and she had to work to produce some approximation of a serene smile to counterbalance it. "A good one, I think. I hope."

"But what kind of queen can you expect to be?" Diana asked, her brows arching high as if astonished Kiara had not raised this issue herself. "You were raised to know about oenology and viticulture, not royal intrigue and matters of state."

"Your faith in me is touching," Kiara said, her smile growing hard to maintain. She stood up then, desperate, suddenly, to avoid getting any deeper into this with her mother. She was afraid of what she might uncover inside herself that she didn't want to know.

Diana only shrugged. "It's not a question of faith," she said. "I talked quite a bit with Queen Madihah at your wedding, you know. She was very open about having been trained to be the king's perfect companion since before she could walk."

Again her dark brows rose. She didn't have to say anything further—it lay there between them as if she'd shouted it.

You are not queen material.

Kiara gathered up her things with as much control as possible, determined not to show Diana how unerring her aim had been, nor how hard she'd managed to strike her target. How did her mother manage to see straight into the heart of her, where she hid her worst fears?

"I don't have time for this," she said as calmly as she could. Which was perhaps not very calm at all. "I have to leave for Khatan early tomorrow. If there's anything else?" She knew her smile was too brittle. "About the business, Mother. Not about my marriage. Please."

"I would just like you to be *realistic* about this, Kiara," Diana said, her flashing brown gaze showing the first hint of emotion Kiara could remember seeing in years. It made her stomach twist, guilt and obligation and something else.

"No, you wouldn't," she replied, temper boiling inside her, rushing in to cover the rest of the things she didn't want to feel. Temper was easier. Cleaner. "You would like me to see things your way. You would like me to *do* things your way."

"Do you imagine that you are the only girl to ever be swept away in some kind of fantasy romance?" Diana retorted. She rose, too, and waved a hand at the window, as if to encompass the vines stretching off toward the hills, the chateau, the whole of their family, their lives, their history. "I was starry-eyed when I met your father, but that hardly prepared me for the reality of running this business, did it? Much less raising a child all on my own when he was gone."

Kiara didn't want to hear this. Not again. This story was imprinted on her bones. It was a story of sacrifice and loss, and then a deep and abiding disappointment that Kiara fell so short of living up to all the things her mother had done for her. Was still doing for her.

It had guided her every step until she'd met Azrin.

"What can any of that possibly matter now?" she asked, her voice low, something dark opening wide inside her that she was afraid to look at too closely. That she knew she needed to close down, hide away, lest it rise up and eat her alive. "I am his wife. His queen. This is happening whether you like it or not, Mother."

Whether you like it or not, too, a small voice whispered inside her—and she immediately hated herself for it. Diana let out a sigh that was loud in the sudden quiet of the office.

"Oh, Kiara," she said, that familiar mix of bafflement and exasperation in her voice, her gaze. And something else—something that made that hard knot inside Kiara seem to swell in response. "None of this is about what *I* want."

Azrin found her out on the private terrace that linked their suites in the family wing of the sprawling palace that sat high on the cliffs above the ancient city of Arjat an-Nahr, where brash skyscrapers now thrust into the skyline along with delicate minarets from centuries past.

She was curled up on one of the deep chaises, her gaze trained out over the dark sea that danced and shimmered far below her. The sun had set but recently, only a line of crimson edged with gold stretched out across the horizon to mark its passing.

Azrin liked that she was here, within reach, mere days since he'd seen her last. The pleasure of it moved through him, so deep and full that the tension of the long day seemed to ease away with every step that brought him closer to her. He liked her here, close by. He'd liked knowing that she had arrived safely and was already in the palace when he finally quit his endless round of meetings and strategy sessions.

She was the single bright spot in a long and complicated day.

She looked over her shoulder toward him as he drew near. There was an expression on her face that he couldn't quite categorize—that he didn't think he'd seen before—but then she smiled. He was already smiling back before he realized that her eyes were darker than they ought to have been.

"I'm glad you're here," he said.

He moved over to the chaise and dropped to sit at the opposite end. The terrace was alive with blooms, bright blossoms by day and the sweet scent of jasmine now that night had fallen. Up above, the stars began to come out. And for a moment, he thought, they could be anyone. Just a woman and a man and the whole night stretched out before them.

He did not allow himself to examine how much he wished that could be true—that they could fall back into that world of pretend they'd lived in all these years. Hidden in, even.

Kiara shifted position against the back of the chaise, and Azrin took the opportunity to arrange her how he wanted her—draping her legs over his lap so he could hold the slender shape of them in his palms. She wore something airy and insubstantial, not quite a dress and not one of her silk wrappers, and her narrow feet were bare. Her hair tumbled around her shoulders, damp from a recent shower, and her face was scrubbed clean of cosmetics.

She was beautiful, and he couldn't understand why she felt so far away when she was right here. When he was touching her.

"How were your meetings?" she asked. Her voice was neutral. Entirely too neutral. He was instantly on guard.

"Much too long," he said. Carefully.

He thought of the bickering ministers, the arguments, the usual pointless intractability from the usual suspects—one of them, sadly, his father. He thought of the inevitable pandering, the concessions, the headaches that were soon to be his alone to deal with. It already felt thankless and dangerous, this relentless push toward progress that he sometimes thought only he supported, and yet there was no stopping it. He had given his word to his people when he was a brash and idealistic twenty-two. He couldn't take it back now, simply because it was harder than he'd anticipated—and happening so much sooner than he'd planned.

And on top of all that was Kiara, with that odd note in her voice and that remote look in her gaze, as if he'd done something to her when all he'd wanted was to talk all of this out. To hear her perspective—to have someone else on his side. He told himself that he was not disappointed, that she had only just arrived. That there was time enough for the kind of conversations he envisioned. That there was no reason to feel so alone.

"Long and complicated," he added, his voice more curt than it should have been.

"Your aide filled me in on your expectations when I arrived," she replied, her voice noticeably less neutral. "At length. And then your sisters took up where he left off." Something flashed in her dark eyes then, and she moved her legs against him, as if restless. "You think I need lessons in etiquette, Azrin? From a battalion of your sisters? Have I humiliated you in the eyes of all the world and you failed to mention it until now?"

He felt as if he had suddenly found himself standing in the middle of a loaded minefield, a sensation he did not care for at all. He'd thought she would appreciate the advice his sisters could give her on how to comport herself like a Khatanian noble. He fought to keep his temper—too close to the surface, after having been sorely tested all day long—at bay.

"You have no formal training in diplomacy,"

he said, forcing his tone into something reasonable. He'd been practicing this very same tone of voice all day long, hadn't he? It should have been as familiar to him as a second skin by now. "My sisters are renowned for their impeccable manners. They are the obvious choice to help you."

He searched her face, looking for the Kiara he knew, always so clever and amused, and seeing only those too-dark eyes looking back at him. Waiting for an explanation of his decision to send his sisters to her that should, he thought with a touch of asperity, have already been obvious to her.

"You will be the queen, Kiara," he said. He told himself he sounded far more patient than he felt. "There are things you'll be expected to know— ways you'll be expected to behave. That's all."

"What's wrong with how I behave now?" Her brows rose, challenging him, but with an unfamiliar darkness there, too. "Is there some embarrassing photograph I don't know about? Some tawdry incident I can't recall?"

"Of course not." He reminded himself that it wasn't her fault that his government was an ancient dinosaur that creaked along, arthritic and demanding, and only he could change it—if it could be changed at all. It wasn't her fault he was out of patience, his temper already frayed too thin. "But you will no longer be a princess who can, to some extent, do as she pleases. You will be the symbol of femininity for all of Khatan." His lips curved. "No pressure, of course."

He wanted her to smile, but her gorgeous mouth remained flat, and he felt it like a slap.

"No pressure," she repeated slowly, as if she was working it out in her head, "yet my current behavior is apparently so deficient you had to send your sisters to me the moment I set foot in the palace. When you'd never mentioned this to me at all. I felt ambushed, Azrin."

He sighed then, all the tension and weariness of the day flooding back into him, the exhaustion of every day since his father's announcement swamping him.

"Will you be one more fire I must put out today, Kiara?" he asked, unable to keep the sharp edge from his voice. "One more problem I must solve?"

She stiffened.

"I thought I was having a conversation with my husband," she said, her voice tight. Like a stranger's. "I didn't realize this was an audience with the king."

His hands tightened around her calves when she would have moved her legs from his lap, but he checked his impatience, and let her go. He watched her as she stood, noting the way she brushed invisible lint from her front with angry hands. She didn't look at him, and he hated it. He hated all of this. He thought of the last time they'd met after a separation, in Sydney.

How had they strayed so far from that night? And so fast?

"I assume there's some dinner we need to get ready for," she murmured.

And, of course, there was. There always was. He would have hated that inevitability, too, but it was futile. This was his life.

But Azrin couldn't abide the distance between them—especially not now, when she was in the palace and would remain here. With him. Not just a musical voice on the telephone, a few funny lines of email to read between meetings. He reached over and snagged her wrist in his hand, tugging her toward him. She came without resistance, though her expression was serious as she gazed down at him. Troubled. He couldn't stand that, either.

He brought her face to his, and kissed her as he'd wanted to do since the moment he'd received the news from his aide that she had arrived at the palace.

He teased, he toyed.

He caressed her and seduced her with every weapon in his arsenal. He licked and tasted that mouth of hers that had obsessed him for so long, kissing her until the tension in her body eased— until she was loose and pliable and she sighed against him. Until there was nothing between them but this heat, this unbankable fire, that he wished they had the time to fully explore. Here, now.

When he finally lifted his head she was sitting in his lap, and her face was flushed and warm.

"I need you to do this with me," he whispered against her mouth fiercely. He pulled back, studied her face, wished he understood this need that raged in him. This pulse of something like fury, something hot and intense. "I need your support, Kiara. Now more than ever."

Her gaze was still so serious, despite the heat

that lingered there. He had the sudden, unpleasant notion that he was missing something—but he dismissed it. Kiara was open. Direct. She would simply tell him if there was something he needed to know. He was sure of it.

Her mouth crooked into that smile that he had loved since the first moment he'd seen it, so long ago now, in the midst of a wet Melbourne afternoon, and he ignored the lingering sense that there was too much reservation behind it tonight. There were too many other things going on around them, he thought. Too much else to do, and surely she understood that.

She would be fine. She always was.

They always were.

"I'm here, aren't I?" she asked quietly, and he told himself it was what he wanted.

That it was enough.

Kiara became public property overnight. As if she, herself, ceased to exist now that she was meant to be queen in a matter of weeks rather than simply *one day*.

And the more she was regarded as something public, something belonging to anyone and everyone, she registered with a rising tide of panic that worsened every day, the more she seemed to disappear beneath the weight of Azrin's crown.

And he wasn't even king yet.

Every day that passed, every long day during which Azrin's many sisters taught Kiara how ill-suited she was to this role of queen and every night which brought Azrin closer to his father's nearly-relinquished throne, Kiara felt more and more as if an unseen hand was closing around her throat. And tightening.

The worst part was, she had no one to talk to about it.

Azrin was so tired, so distracted. *Overwhelmed,* she thought, and she told herself she understood it. She didn't want to hear him heave another heavy sigh and tell her she was one more fire to put out, did she? She didn't want to be another burden to him. She wanted anything but that, in fact.

And in truth, she didn't know how to raise this sort of issue with him anyway.

They had always been on the same page before now, more or less. They'd fought, as all couples did, but they had always been the sort of fights brought on by stress and exhaustion and too much travel—a short tone or a snapped reply that bloomed into temper, and the resultant hurt feelings that could easily be soothed by a conversation and delicious, reconciliatory sex.

Kiara didn't think that would work this time. What could she say? *It hurts my feelings that you expect me to be your queen? Let's see if we can solve that with a chat?* Of course not.

She couldn't contact the friends she'd become less close with over the years, when what little free time she'd had was filled with Azrin. Her friendships had become little more than the odd catch-up telephone call, a well-received email here and there and happy photographs in the usual online places. Kiara couldn't imagine how she could turn that around now. She would hardly know where to start. And any coworkers she might think to confide in were far too likely to drop hints of any unrest to Diana, and Kiara couldn't bear the idea that she might prove her mother right about her marriage.

She wished she were less proud. More than that, she wished her stoic, loving grandmother were still alive and still able to make the world feel right again with a simple hug, no matter what might have happened.

Azrin had never felt further away, for all that he was geographically closer than he'd been in years. The bittersweet irony of that ate at her. And meanwhile Kiara felt as if she was disappearing under the onslaught of some relentless tide, bit by bit, until she wondered what would be left of her at all.

"It would be better if you were pregnant," King Zayed announced one night, scowling at her from his place at the head of the table.

His words cast an immediate and total hush over the marvelous long table that commanded pride of place in the ornate room of the palace that was only used for private family meals, silencing all the members of the royal family who had gathered around it.

Who all, of course, turned to stare directly at Kiara, in case she was in any doubt about who the old king was addressing.

She was in no doubt. She simply felt sick.

Beside her, she felt Azrin tense, but he remained silent, though she could feel that dark current running through him, humming beneath his skin. She was afraid to look at him—afraid that if she did, she would see that he was as appalled as she was by this and would then be unable to govern herself appropriately.

And more afraid by far that he would not be appalled at all.

"That *would* be ideal," one of King Zayed's highest ministers, who was married to one of Azrin's sisters, agreed at once, as if this was a plan he could launch into action with the force of his agreement.

"The country loves it when the royal family is expecting a child," Queen Madihah chimed in. She aimed her usual calm smile at Kiara. "Especially when it's the queen."

Kiara managed, somehow, to keep from letting her fork drop from her nerveless fingers to clatter against the side of her plate. Or from throwing it at the king.

"Unfortunately," she said when the silence dragged on, when it became clear that Azrin was not planning to speak to his father on her behalf, when she thought she might die if everyone kept staring at her like that and some part of her wished she would, "I am not."

She was so upset she shook slightly, even hours later when she and Azrin returned to their rooms together.

"Why didn't you say something?" she asked.

It took everything she had not to scream at him. Not to simply scream out all the things she was feeling inside, that she was afraid to even look at too closely for fear that even giving them names would allow them to take her over and suck her under, never to be seen again.

"What was there to say?" He did not pretend he didn't know what she was talking about. He shrugged, his expression almost forbidding. "He is still the king. He will always be my father."

"This is *my body*." Kiara shook her head, bewildered. Still feeling something very near to violated by all those eyes on her, all that attention to something that should have been hers and Azrin's alone. "It's *private*."

He looked at her for a long moment, a certain hardness in his gaze that she had never seen before. It made a pit in her stomach open, then gape wide.

"No," he said eventually. She had the impression he was choosing his words carefully, and that hurt too, as if they had become complete strangers to each other in a few short weeks. *As if*, something treacherous and terrified whispered deep within her, *you never knew each other at all*. "It isn't."

She blinked. "What are you talking about?"

"The heir to the kingdom of Khatan will come from your body," he said, his fierce attention dropping to her abdomen as if he could *see* the babies they'd never talked about in concrete terms, always couching it in *someday* and *when we're ready* language.

Kiara's hands crept over her own belly, whether to protect herself or in response to something far more primitive, she didn't know.

"And the sooner that heir exists, the sooner the whole country can breathe a collective sigh of relief," he continued in that same aloof tone. "They are still outraged that I vowed to take only one wife. What if you cannot produce sons? What if the royal line is lost?"

Azrin shrugged and then smiled, and Kiara almost smiled back, because what he was saying was so archaic that it couldn't possibly apply to her. To them. To their life together.

But then she remembered that it did.

"Until all these questions are answered," he said, "I'm afraid your body will be seen to be as much theirs as yours."

"And you accept that," she said softly.

"This is our life, Kiara," he replied, that exhausted sort of look in his eyes that made her feel small and petulant. But that was unfair, wasn't it? This was her life, too. "This is who we are."

This is who you are, she thought, but did not say.

She moved away from him, sinking down to sit in one of the heavily brocaded armchairs, blinking back a searing heat, determined that she would not cry. Not now, when she already felt too vulnerable.

"And maybe they're right," Azrin said after a moment. Kiara felt the world tilt beneath her feet, and she wasn't even standing. She stared at him, unable, in that moment, to speak. He shrugged out of his clothes, baring his beautiful body to her, and for once she felt almost numb. "Maybe we should start thinking about children."

She swallowed, panic licking over her skin, making her head feel heavy.

"Are you saying that as my husband?" she asked, her voice hardly above a whisper. "Or as the king who agrees with his mother that it would foster goodwill with your subjects?"

His gaze grew cold. Unbearably hard. "Can't I be both?"

She didn't know how to answer that. She didn't understand what was happening. She only knew she wanted to curl into a ball and sob, and none of this was helping.

"You told me we could wait until I was ready," she reminded him, a kind of thick dread making her limbs feel heavy. Making her temples pound. "You promised."

"Don't look at me like that, Kiara," he replied, his tone harsh. Or maybe it only felt that way, like one more blow in a long series of them. "We've been married for five years. You know I must have an heir at some point or another. It's not entirely unreasonable to discuss it, is it?"

"Maybe you and your parents and your cabinet ministers should consult with each other, then," she threw at him, feeling wild. Miserable.

Attacked. "You can let me know what conclusions you reach. I'll just trot along, obeying your decrees like a happy little brood mare, shall I?"

She regretted it the moment she said it.

His gaze turned dark, and his face seemed to tighten. He stared at her, affront and something worse all over him, and Kiara couldn't seem to do anything but stare back. He muttered something in Arabic that made her flinch even without understanding it, then turned and strode away from her. She heard the water turn on in the adjacent bath, and only then did she let herself breathe, though it sounded more like a sob in the simmering wake of his exit.

A wave of misery flooded through her, and she couldn't stand it. She couldn't even seem to breathe through it. She found herself up and on her feet, then walking into Azrin's bath without knowing she meant to move.

She found him in the shower, steam billowing, bracing himself against the tiled wall as the water beat down on him from above. He turned to look at her as she opened the glass door, and her heart seemed to thud too hard against her ribs.

His eyes were much too dark. His mouth was

grim. She felt both reverberate deep inside of her, ripping at her.

"I am not your enemy," he bit out, as if this hurt him, too. As if she did. "Why do you want so badly to be mine?"

But she didn't want to talk. She didn't know what to say that wouldn't hurt them both.

She stepped into the shower fully clothed, and let the hot water wash into her. Over her, wetting her dress, her hair. She put her hands out to touch his slick, hard chest, and when he shifted as if he wanted to talk rather than touch, she gave in to the helpless need clawing at her and slid down to her knees. Slicking her hair back, she knelt before him and kissed her way over the hard ridges of his abdomen, then farther down, her hands gripping the hard muscles of his thighs.

And somewhere along the way she forgot that she meant to quiet him, to apologize somehow, and simply found herself worshiping him. Tasting him. Testing those delicious muscles, that mesmerizing skin, with her mouth, her hands, her tongue.

When she finally moved to his sex, he was hard and inviting, and when she leaned back to look up at him his eyes seemed to glitter with the same tension she felt inside of her. That familiar burn, with a new, desperate edge.

She reached between his legs, letting her hands caress the heavy weight of him, and then she leaned forward and took him deep in her mouth. He said her name like a prayer.

And slowly, deliberately, using her lips and her tongue and the long, slow strokes she knew drove him crazy, Kiara made them both forget.

At least for now.

The night before he took the throne, they hardly slept.

He came into her again and again. He laid her out on the wide bed in the center of his room and stretched out above her, loving his way over every single inch of her skin. She shattered into pieces, he followed. She screamed his name until she thought she might go hoarse.

She took him in and loved him back and neither of them spoke of the desperation, the ferocity, that drove him so hard, that made him near-in-exhaustible, that made her eyes well over as she clung to him. That made his mouth seem very nearly grim, even in passion.

That made her wish, so fiercely, that she could take them back to where they'd been before his father's announcement, that she could will away the dawn and everything that she knew would come with it.

But it came anyway, inevitably. A whole nation waited for him. Monarchs and presidents, emirs and prime ministers and cheering crowds of his own people were there to pay their respects to the new King of Khatan. And Kiara would walk slightly behind him, as was tradition, bow her head, accept her own crown and become his queen.

She wondered in that last, stolen moment in their bedroom if he would ever truly be hers again. If he ever had been—or if all of this had simply been borrowed time, after all. She cast the unsettling thought aside. She made herself smile. For him.

All of this was for him. And she doubted he had any idea how hard this was for her, how deeply she feared losing herself entirely to his crown, his country.

Even harder than that was her suspicion that it was something he wouldn't want to know.

"We must go," he said. His voice was too gruff, and there were shadows in his nearly-blue eyes. Kiara did not want to be one of them. Not today. "We must be dressed and prepared and moved into place, like pieces on a chess board."

She ran her hands up over his perfect chest, tilted her head back to look at him, and felt the first real smile she'd had in ages move over her mouth. She did not want to think of her endless lessons in etiquette from the disapproving collective of his sisters, all of whom had made it clear that she could never be the queen he needed. She did not want to think about how cold he had become, how distant. How far away. She did not want to think of chess, either. She wanted to love him, as simple as that. That was all she'd ever wanted.

"The next time we are alone," she said softly, "you will be the king."

She did not say *my king*.

"I will be your husband," he replied, pressing a last kiss to her temple, soft and sweet, making her ache for him. For them. For their perfect past and their uncertain future. "Nothing more and nothing less."

And she wanted, so desperately, to believe him.

CHAPTER FOUR

SOME two months after his grand coronation, Azrin escorted his queen with great fanfare and a pervasive sense of relief into a glittering ball-room in Washington, D.C.

Other couples took honeymoons, but the brand-new King and Queen of Khatan had traveled purely to allow Azrin to have long-overdue state visits and hold talks with Khatan's allies around the globe. He had spent a few hours in the Oval Office this afternoon discussing his plans to transition his kingdom toward a constitutional monarchy, and now it was time to make nice with the diplomats. This was the final stop on this particular political tour, and tomorrow they could finally go back home to Khatan.

He could hardly wait.

"You look beautiful," he murmured in Kiara's ear, and she smiled, though she didn't turn into him as she might have once. He felt his eyes narrow.

He was impatient for some kind of real privacy, finally. He wanted to be alone with her, rather than surrounded on all sides by too many people wanting too much of him, day and night. He wanted to lose himself in her without worrying if the walls were thin and the Royal Guard too close—or if he would be called away to some crisis, some call, some piece of news that could not wait for morning.

She looked impossibly regal tonight as she greeted the assembled dignitaries before them in a gown of rich burgundy, her hair piled high on the top of her head in a complicated arrangement and surrounded with sparkling diamonds that caught the light with her every movement. She laughed politely at something one of the portly, tuxedoed men said to her and he realized, suddenly, that he couldn't recall the last time he'd heard her real laughter—that gorgeous laugh of hers that made him feel as if he basked in the sunshine of it. Of her.

One more thing that needed to change, he

thought. One more thing these long, grueling months had taken from them both.

Once through the receiving line, Azrin led her out onto the dance floor and pulled her into his arms. She swayed toward him gracefully, her posture achingly perfect as he led her in the steps of the dance. He gazed down into her face and saw, he thought with a pang, his queen. Smooth, gracious. Perfect. But not his Kiara.

"Do you remember that weekend in Barcelona?" he asked suddenly. Without thought—only the need to reach her, somehow.

She blinked in that way that he was beginning to recognize as a stalling tactic—one that he suspected kept that irreverent tongue of hers under control. He knew he should have been pleased that she'd learned discretion. Hadn't that been why she'd spent all those weeks with his sisters? But instead he felt something entirely too much like loss.

"Which weekend?" she asked lightly. Far too politely, as if he was one of the dignitaries she'd just charmed with so little effort and even less of the real her he knew lurked in there somewhere.

It had to. "We've been there any number of times over the years."

"You know which one." He could not pull her close the way he wanted to, and he could not have said why her reticence irritated him so much, so suddenly. He ordered himself to relax. "But I will remind you. We drank far too much sangria and danced for hours. We were the youngest couple in the place by several decades." He moved closer than he should. "And I know you remember it as well as I do."

He remembered her laughter most of all—the way it had poured over them both like water, bathing them both in the joy of it. He remembered the insistent pulse of the music and the fact that they had been soundly out danced by local couples old enough to be his own grandparents. And he remembered walking back to their hotel in the small hours, holding her hand in his and her impractical shoes in the other, as if the streets were theirs alone. He smiled at the memory.

And then she met his gaze, her brown eyes so serious, and his smile faded.

"I remember," she said.

An odd note in her voice made everything go very still inside him.

"Something is the matter." It was more a statement of fact than a question. His hand tightened a fraction around hers. "What is it?"

She shook her head slightly.

"This is hardly the time or the place to talk about anything serious," she said. She indicated the Washington elite surrounding them on all sides, all polite chatter and sharp speculation, with a tilt of her head.

"If that is meant to make me believe that something is *not* wrong," he pointed out, his gaze narrow on hers, "it has failed. Miserably."

She only shook her head again, and smiled that perfect, empty smile. And what could Azrin do? He was the King of Khatan. There was no scenario in which he could have any kind of intimate conversation with his wife in the middle of a dance floor. He couldn't even kiss her the way he wanted to without causing the sort of commotion he preferred to avoid.

He found he hated it.

But he waited.

And as he waited, he watched her, feeling as

if he somehow hadn't seen her in a long time, though they had traveled all over the world together in these past weeks, with the whole of their necessary entourage. She was pale beneath her expertly applied cosmetics. And there was a certain kind of brittleness about the way she moved.

"Are you ill?" he asked abruptly when they were finally alone in a suite set aside for visiting heads of state in an exclusive Georgetown hotel, all rich, old wood and faint gestures toward something more art deco.

Kiara stopped walking away from him—toward the master bedroom at the far end of the suite and the sumptuous bath, presumably—her gown whispering around her as she turned back to face him. He watched her for a moment from his position at the top of the steps that led down from the formal foyer into the long, elegant room, trying to see behind that smooth mask he realized she'd been wearing for weeks now.

Trying to understand how she could feel so far away when she was right there, within reach. The tension between them pulled taut, making the vast room seem to contract around them. He hated that, too.

"Of course I'm not ill," she said, her forehead allowing the slightest frown.

"Pregnant?" He didn't know why he'd asked that. To poke at her?

He could see her swallow almost convulsively as he walked down the steps, closing the distance between them. Her mouth flattened. Her eyes flashed with what he took to be temper, but at least it was better than that mask.

"No. Still not pregnant, should you care to alert the media."

"If there is something wrong—" he began, hearing the impatience in his own voice and unable, somehow, to curtail it.

"What could be wrong?" Her eyes were too bright. She turned her head as if she wanted to hide it, looking out toward the brick terrace that stretched the length of the suite on the other side of the glass windows, the rooftops of Georgetown spread out before them. Deceptively inviting, Azrin thought darkly, in such a deceitful city. "You are a success by any measure. You have been hailed as an innovative and modernizing force for good in a troubled region. A worthy successor to your father in every respect. Surely all of this has turned out exactly as you wanted. As you planned."

"Kiara."

He didn't know what he wanted. He didn't feel like any kind of success, not when she looked away from him, when she seemed so closed off, so far away. He didn't know what moved inside of him, tearing at him. He only knew he couldn't stand this. Whatever this was.

"What else can you possibly want?" she asked him, her voice the faintest whisper. *From me*, he thought she added, but he couldn't be sure. And he didn't know he meant to move until his hands were on her shoulders and his mouth was hard against hers.

"I want you," he growled. He tasted salt and something else, something bitter, but beyond that was simply Kiara, and it took so very little of her to make him drunk. "I always want you."

He dragged his hands through her hair, scattering the diamonds that had nestled there, digging his fingers into the long tresses, holding her still as he took. Tasted. And took some more.

He was desperate then, and she met him with her own heat, turning his own mad desire back on him—sending them both higher. Hotter. She tugged his coat from his shoulders, his shirt from his trousers. He unhooked her from her gown with more determination than finesse, and then she was pushing him down on the nearest sofa. He twisted her beneath him, settling himself between her thighs as they wrestled off what remained of their clothing and then he found his way into the molten core of her, thrusting hard. Deep.

She gasped, arching up against him, locking her long, smooth legs tight around his hips. He exulted in the heat of her, the lush softness. The perfect fit. The way her hips rose to meet his, then rolled in that particular way that was all Kiara. All his.

He slowed, brushing her hair back from her face and waiting for her eyes to open, to focus on him.

"Tell me what's wrong," he said.

But she only moved her hips against him, her ankles locked in the small of his back. He leaned down and pulled one of her tight, hard nipples into his mouth, making her laugh and then moan.

"Tell me," he said again, and then began to

move, his strokes measured and deep, making her shudder against him.

"I've told you in a thousand ways," she said, her voice uneven, her body arching to meet his thrusts. "You need to learn how to listen."

So he listened. He took her other nipple in his mouth, reached down between them to the place where they were joined, and with a single sure touch, threw her right over the edge.

And then he did it all over again.

And again.

Until, he was sure, nothing at all could ever matter but this.

When he woke, it was morning.

He pulled on the nearest thing he could find and made his way out into the long living area of the suite. He found her fully dressed in one of her elegant day dresses and standing by the windows in the great room. She held her morning cup of coffee between her hands, her eyes fixed out the window again, as if the rooftops opposite held secrets she was determined to solve.

"We will not fly out for another few hours," he said, his voice still raspy from sleep. And the lack of it. He was happier than he perhaps should be that the tour was finally over, that he could revel in this morning, empty of his aides and his responsibilities, for now. He leaned down to press a kiss to the back of her neck. "Come back to bed."

"I can't," she said. Then a small sound, as if she sucked in a breath. "I'm not going back to Khatan with you."

"Where are you going?" He felt lazy. Indulgent.

He helped himself to her coffee, pulling the heavy ceramic mug from her hand and taking a pull of it before handing it back to her. She set it down on a nearby accent table and then looked at him, her gaze unreadable.

"Australia."

He nodded absently and turned back toward the bedroom, rubbing a hand over his jaw. He was thinking of the shower, and how good the hot water would feel against his skin. He was wondering how long he could keep any outside thoughts at bay this morning, after such a long and satisfying night—how long he could pretend he was nothing more than a man. Not a king at all today. Not yet.

"Are you planning to visit your mother?" he asked over his shoulder. "When will you return?"

She didn't respond. He turned again, to find her watching him with an expression he didn't recognize on her pretty face. Resigned, perhaps. Some mix of sadness and something else, something like defiance.

"What is it?" he asked, on alert again.

"That's just it, Azrin," she said. "I don't know that I will return."

If it had not been for that terrible, arrested look on his face, the sudden stillness in his powerful body, Kiara might have thought she hadn't spoken out loud.

"I need some time," she said.

She wasn't sure, now, if it was some newfound strength or simple desperation that had chased her from their bed this morning, got her to stop her silent, pointless sobbing in the shower, and wait for him here. Much less actually say what she'd wanted to say for weeks now. She wasn't sure it mattered either way.

She let out the breath she'd been holding, closed her eyes and finished it. "I want a separation."

There was a beat. Then another. Her heart pounded so hard inside her chest that it actually hurt.

"What did you say to me?"

Her eyes snapped to his. They glittered dangerously. He looked particularly wild this morning, his dark hair mussed from sleep, his jaw unshaven, and only those trousers low on his narrow hips. His voice was the iciest she'd ever heard it, a frigid sort of growl that sliced into her like a blade. She had the panicked thought that if she looked down, she would see her own blood.

But she didn't look. She didn't dare. She couldn't tear her gaze away from his. She couldn't do anything but stand there, frozen solid while he seemed to expand to fill the room and she was forced to remember that he was a dangerous, impossibly lethal man.

He only pretended to be tame, she reminded herself, feeling breathless and faintly ill, because it suited him to do so.

"I can't possibly have heard you correctly," he said, his voice that same cold lash.

He didn't move closer to her, but then, he didn't have to. She could see every long, hard line of his big body, so dangerously still, all of that un-compromising male power coiled in him. *Ready.* Sex and command. It was so heady, so intoxicating, that she understood with no little despair that she would always want it—want *him*—no matter how miserable it might make her.

But this was what men like Azrin did. They commanded. They ruled. They blocked out the whole world. They *took*. What had ever made her think she could stand strong and independent, her own person, next to this much power and force? She'd been lucky he'd let her play around in the fantasy of it all this time.

Lucky, she repeated to herself, and it almost made her cry.

"Are you planning to say something else?" he asked, in that dark, impatient tone that made her stomach turn over, hard, even as she felt too hot, too cold. "Am I to draw my own conclusions about this time you need? This separation? Or, let me guess, you are laboring under the delusion that I'll just let you run back to Australia without a fight?"

"I am not happy," Kiara said then, finally, simply, and the words seemed to crack something open inside of her. As if she'd been afraid to say them, afraid to admit that she felt them, afraid of what would happen once she did…

This, she thought then, wishing she could feel numb. Wishing this could simply be over somehow. Wishing that she had never sat down at that café table all those years ago. *This was exactly what she was afraid of.*

"Are you sure?" His voice was so dark, with such a vicious kick beneath. "You seemed happy enough every time you came in my arms last night. I lost count, Kiara. How many times was it?"

Some sickening mix of temper and desperation swirled in her belly and then pulled tight, giving her just enough false courage to lift her chin, square her shoulders and figure out some way to push the necessary words out of her mouth.

"Yes, Azrin," she said. "You're very good in bed. Congratulations. But that isn't the point, is it?"

He spread his hands out as if in surrender, and she had the despairing thought that he'd never looked less like a supplicant. Even a gesture like this made him look like what he was—a bloody king, indulging her. Patronizing her, on some level, whether he knew it or not.

"Why don't you tell me what the point is," he suggested, and there was less ice in his voice now and more of that deliberate, measured calmness that she found she hated. It smacked of that same indulgence. "You are the one who wants to separate." He said that last word as if it was a vile curse.

"I have done nothing for the past three months but trail around after you," Kiara said, evenly. Rationally. The way she delivered reports in business meetings. "First there was the pre-coronation finishing school with your sisters. Then the months of appearances. Always smiling. Always dignified and silent and polite, entirely without opinions on anything except the flowers. The decor. The weather. That is not what I want from my life."

"That is your job," he said, shrugging, though his eyes remained hard on hers.

"It is *your* job," she retorted, still fighting to keep her voice as calm as she knew it needed to be. "I have an entirely different job, as you know very well. It does not involve acting as if I am nothing more than a repository for opinions you have already vetted. A figure, nothing more. Or, even better, a currently empty uterus that your whole country gets a say in filling, apparently. My actual job involves my *brain*."

His eyes were so dark now, too dark, and seemed to bore into her, seeing all kinds of things she was sure she'd rather keep private. Hidden. But she didn't look away. She knew this was a fight for her life. She knew it with a certainty that should have scared her—that *had* scared her so much that she'd gone almost entirely mute these last weeks rather than risk these words slipping out at some state dinner and shaming them both in front of the whole world.

And because she hadn't wanted this, she admitted to herself. She hadn't wanted to believe that this was happening, even as every day she saw less and less of herself in the mirror.

"I can't believe that you honestly think the Queen of Khatan should—or could—be the vice president of a foreign corporation in her spare time." Azrin's voice was dark and curt.

He shook his head, an impatient expression moving over that ruthless face and telling her quite clearly that he was not taking her seriously. That he had already relegated her to just one more of those daily fires of his, just one more problem to solve. She told herself she shouldn't let it hurt as much as it did. That this—exactly this—was precisely why she had to take this step.

"I don't think you truly think so, either," he continued in the same tone. "I think your feelings are hurt. My attention has been on my responsibilities and you feel ignored. Hence this tantrum."

"This isn't what I signed up for," she said, though it cost her to keep so calm. "And it isn't a tantrum to say so. Pretending that this is a childish display of temper so you don't have to deal with what I'm saying, however, very well might be."

"When you met me I was the Crown Prince of Khatan," Azrin said, the chill back in his voice, that terrible steel in his eyes. "This is, in fact, *exactly* what you signed up for." He laughed slightly, though there was no humor in it. "Sooner than we planned, perhaps, but that's life. Plans change. Sometimes you simply have to do your duty."

"You're talking about *your* life," she said through the constriction in her chest, which she was deathly afraid were the tears she refused to cry. Not in front of him. Not when it was so important he take her seriously. That he *listen*. "*Your* duty. What about mine?"

"What about it?" he asked, every inch of him so arrogant. So incredulous. "This *is* your life, Kiara. Whatever games we played over the past five years, this is reality. The sooner you accept it, the happier you'll be."

And there it was, she thought dully. Painfully. Had she known all along that it would come to this? Had she felt it somehow? Was that why all the pressure to have a baby had rubbed her the wrong way—because she knew this was only a game to him after all?

"Were you playing games all this time?" she asked, unable to keep the catch from her voice. "Because I wasn't. I have my own responsibilities. My own duties. There are people depending on me, too—"

"I am talking about a kingdom," Azrin said, that impatient edge in his voice again, that cold fury in his gaze. "A government. A country. A whole population. You are talking about grapes."

She felt as if he'd hit her. That dismissive tone in his voice. That look in his eyes. The proof that he had never supported her the way he'd pretended to—that their relationship was nothing but a lie. She felt empty. Hollowed out.

Or, if she was brutally honest, she only wished she did.

How she wished she did.

"No," she said, astonished that she could even speak. Much less manage to sound so calm. So unmoved and unbothered. As if none of this was breaking her heart. "You're talking about your family—and I'm talking about mine."

The silence stretched out between them, ripe with all the things he had to prevent himself from saying. That deliberately even tone of hers slapped at him, infuriated him. Azrin had to fight to keep his temper under control.

"What do you want, Kiara?" he asked when he was certain he could speak without shouting. "How do you see this working out? I am the

King of Khatan. You are the Queen. That can't be changed, no matter where you choose to hide."

"I don't know," she said, her voice still so frustratingly even, despite the edge in his. It made him feel wild inside. He saw her hands had balled into fists at her sides, and comforted himself with the knowledge that she was not nearly as cold nor calm as she appeared.

"Do you really think the people will support their queen's sudden residency in Australia?" He eyed her as if she was a stranger instead of the woman who had bewitched him for years, who he still wanted, even when he was this furious with her, even when he had no idea what to do with all this hopeless rage. "Or is that what you want—that kind of scandal?"

"I said I don't know."

Her head jerked up, and her brown eyes looked very nearly black. He could sense her temper more than see it, and he didn't know what was wrong with him that he should want to goad her into exploding. Into showing him what was beneath all of these impossible, terrible things she was saying, none of which he could believe. Much less accept.

"But by all means, you should keep pushing me about it in that aggressive tone of voice," she said. "I'm sure that will clear everything up."

He realized he was gritting his teeth when his jaw began to ache.

"I will never divorce you," he said softly. Deliberately. "Just so we understand each other."

"You don't get to decide that, Azrin," she retorted, frustration bleeding into the even tone of her voice then. She reached up to massage her temples, as if he was a headache she wanted to rub away. "If I want to end this marriage, I will."

"I see." He moved closer to her without meaning to move, until he was near enough that her scent teased at him, that he could hear the catch in her breath as she eyed him warily. Too warily. And still, none of it was enough. None of this made sense. "So you feel that the promises you made, your vows, are only something you have to keep if and when it's convenient for you. Is that what this is?"

"I have done nothing *but* keep my promises!" she snapped at him, and he saw a hectic color bloom across her cheekbones. He should not have been so small a man as to feel that like a victory. "You can't say the same. You married *me*, not some Khatanian paragon, crafted from the cradle to serve your every need. You married me knowing exactly who I was—"

"So did you," he retorted. He shook his head as if that might clear it. "What *is* this? You've hardly spoken to me in weeks—"

"You made it perfectly clear that there was no discussion to be had!" She threw the words at him, cutting him off, a bright fury in her brown eyes.

"Are you referring to the many conversations we've had about your unhappiness?" he gritted out. "Of course not, because you've never mentioned it until now. Yet somehow I am to blame because it was never discussed?"

For a moment, they only stared at each other. He could hear the harsh way she breathed, could see the bright heat on her cheeks and the pallor beneath. He wanted to touch her, to soothe her, to *remind* her—but something in the way she looked at him stopped him.

"You should have known better," she said after a long moment, and the rich, deep pain in her voice nearly undid him. A toxic cocktail of shame and blame and anger ripped through him, too much like weakness. "You knew what kind of wife you needed. You should never have pretended it could be me."

He heard the layers of agony in her words. He felt it in the way she looked at him, in the tears that spilled from her dark eyes that she jabbed at with her hands. And he had no idea what to do to fix this, to change it.

"It is you," he said. He let out a hollow sort of laugh. "It is only you."

She shook her head then, looking, if possible, even more miserable.

"Maybe that's the solution," she said. She lifted her chin as if bracing herself. "Maybe you should stop fighting your heritage and your traditions and simply take a more appropriate wife in addition to me. Or two, just like your father."

For a moment it was as if some white-hot kind of electric charge seared through him, so furious did that remark make him. But he reined it in. He shoved it down. Somehow.

"You want a harem, Kiara?" he asked through his teeth. "I will be more than happy to provide you with one. But let's make sure you're clear on how it works. I get to have as many wives as I want. You get to obey me."

"Or, alternatively, I could divorce you and marry Harry Thompson the way my mother always wanted me to," she snapped back, wholly uncowed by him. "He's never been so appealing, frankly."

"Try it," Azrin suggested, his tone nothing short of murderous. "I dare you. See what happens."

Her brown eyes flashed. "Don't threaten me."

And something seemed to crack inside him. He couldn't control the temper that crashed through him, over him. Not anymore. Not when she was so determined to break him into pieces. Not when he no longer seemed to care if she did.

"Don't threaten *me*, Kiara!" He only realized he was shouting when he heard his own voice, so very loud was it. So raw. Her face paled, but he couldn't seem to stop. "Harems? Divorce? *Harry Thompson?* Will you say anything at all to hurt me?"

She had never heard Azrin raise his voice. Ever.

His temper, she would have said, was a cold

thing. Layers of ice and that cutting edge in his voice. Not this wild, pulsing fury that still echoed from the walls. That shook her, hard and deep, from the inside out. She had to fight to keep a terrified sort of sob inside, and the worst part was, he had no idea how badly she wanted to take it all back. To fall into bed with him, to smile on command when they were out of bed, and pretend that this wasn't killing her, bit by inexorable bit.

He had no idea how much it cost her to do this. He never would.

"I need to think," she said, no longer caring if her voice was uneven. If the tears fell. "I can't do it in Khatan. I can't do it near you. I need to clear my head."

She didn't realize how hard she was crying until she heard her own voice, thick and distorted with her own sobs.

"Kiara…" He looked at her, his eyes so dark and so raw, and she hated that she'd done this to him. That she hadn't been able to simply handle all of these changes, what they meant, no matter how difficult. That she couldn't love him enough to justify losing herself.

But she couldn't. She just couldn't.

Did that mean she'd never really loved him as she should have? What else *could* it mean? And that, she thought dimly, was entirely on her. It was exactly what she had to figure out.

"Space," she managed to say, though the room was full of darkness and damage and she wasn't sure she could survive this. "You need to give me space."

"What will that accomplish?" His voice was little more than a growl. "We've hardly spoken in weeks and this is the conclusion you've drawn. What will space do but confirm it?" His troubled gaze met hers. "Unless, of course, that's what you want."

"You never gave me any space at all, did you?" She shook her head, stepping away from him as if to underscore it. "You argued me into dating you. You talked me into sleeping with you. You convinced me to marry you—"

"Spare me the revisionist history, please," he interrupted, his voice little more than a dangerous rasp. "You are no malleable little puppet. You wanted me then. You want me now." His gaze raked over her, into her. "You're standing three feet away from me with your arms crossed in front of you because you can't trust yourself. You know that if I moved any closer—if I touched you—I'd be inside you and *space* would be the very last thing on your mind."

Kiara didn't realize he'd backed her across the room until she felt one of the sofas behind her. She reached out and held on to it, because she was afraid of what she would do if she didn't— because he was right. She wanted to touch him. She always did.

And look where it had got them.

"Yes," she whispered. "We have sex. Maybe that's all we have."

He let out a breath then, jagged and coarse. He moved closer, and it was too much, as it was always too much. She could feel the power and the anger in him, and worse, all of the pain. And still, he was so beautiful. So fierce, so powerful. Her impossible, addictive attraction to him moved in her like some kind of fever. Even now.

He leaned in, holding her hands in his, and then angled his big body down to rest his forehead against hers. Kiara closed her eyes, and it was as if he surrounded her. Completely.

This was killing her.

"You are the only woman I have ever loved," he said quietly.

And she wanted to die.

But even in that moment, even as her mind spun with a thousand ways she could try to stay and make this work, she knew she couldn't do it. She couldn't disappear any further, or she'd disappear for good. She knew it.

She could feel that intoxicating heat of his, like some kind of fire that burned forever beneath his skin. Enveloping her. Encouraging her to simply lean forward and lose herself in him. She tilted her head back to look up at him, but they were still so close. Close enough to kiss. Close enough that it felt as if they already were.

"If you love me, Azrin," she whispered, because she was desperate. Because she didn't know how else to do this. "Let me go."

He looked at her for a very long time. Kiara wasn't sure either one of them breathed. He took her hands in his, and for a moment she thought he would simply ignore her—simply take her mouth with his and make them both forget. They both knew he could. Some part of her even wanted him to do it, to take this decision out of her hands altogether.

She remembered how she'd loved it once, that he'd made her feel so weak, so overwhelmed, so utterly lost in him. So fascinated. It had been such a contrast to the rest of her life. And she wasn't sure she loved it anymore, but she could feel that same fascination, that same invitation to lose herself in him, as much a part of her now as her own flesh, her own bones. The threat of him as much within her as without.

She understood in that moment that if he did not let her go, she would not be able to make herself leave him. It made her feel hollow inside, that betrayal of herself, but she knew it was true.

And it was amazing how much that part of her wanted him to do it. To make her stay.

"Leave, then," he said, in a voice she hardly recognized, though it broke what was left of her heart into dust.

And then he opened up his hands and let her go.

CHAPTER FIVE

IT WAS shaping up to be a good grape-harvesting season, Kiara told herself with forced cheer as she walked down to breakfast. Despite the fact she'd missed so much of it while she'd been *off playing queen of the castle*, as her mother called it. But it was not even remotely soothing to think about Diana, so Kiara thought about the grapes instead.

When she'd arrived home nearly a month before, they'd been picking the Tempranillo. The grapes were in barrels now, on their way to becoming another excellent Frederick Winery vintage, while the winery turned its attention to the picking of what promised to be a particularly complex and alluring Shiraz.

This was what she was good at, she reminded herself. Grapes and wine. Color, nose and palate. She was home, finally. She was where she belonged. Everything was exactly as it should be, exactly as she'd wanted it.

So why did she feel like a zombie?

She walked, she talked. Kiara was still the vice president of Frederick Winery, but her commitments and tasks had been farmed out to her co-workers when she'd left for Khatan, and there was no way to reclaim her duties without coming clean about the state of her marriage. Luckily, as she'd discovered in her months as queen, she was very good at pretending. She smiled, she laughed, she *acted* as if everything was fine. As if she was on holiday, perhaps.

But inside… Inside she was deathly afraid that there was nothing left of her at all.

Every day, she thought it would be better. Even the littlest bit. She thought she would wake up and feel all that pressure, all that pain, ease. Or at least shift, somehow. She thought she would start to go, say, even five minutes without replaying every word Azrin had said to her in Washington, without seeing that utterly bleak, destroyed look in his stormy eyes. If she could make it through a night without dreaming of him—his breathtaking touch, the sensual thrill of his voice, that approving light in his nearly blue gaze when he looked at her and smiled… But it never happened.

She was beginning to wonder if it ever would.

Through the high, graceful windows that arched along the stairway toward the lower floors of the chateau, Kiara caught the familiar sight of the landscape that had always dominated her life. The lush Frederick vineyards stretched off toward the hills, everything green and gold, in the height of a perfect Barossa Valley summer. This was home, she told herself again. This was not an ancient palace in a foreign city, ripe with ineffable traditions and too many arcane roles she was destined to fail at fulfilling. This was precisely where she belonged. She should be happy—and if not happy, at the very least, content.

And yet she still felt nothing but empty.

Diana was in the kitchen when Kiara entered, looking as casually elegant as ever as she sipped her morning coffee and read the morning paper at the long, wooden table that was the focal point of the bright, cheery room. Kiara's grandmother had made the serviceable kitchen over into the warm center of the great house it was now, and Kiara's girlhood had involved long hours sitting at the table while her gran puttered about at the stove. Diana had made the chateau into a show-piece—somehow unpretentious and luxurious at once, just as she was—but she'd left the kitchen as it was.

Not that it comforted Kiara today. She smiled a polite *good morning* at her mother and then went to fix herself a large cup of coffee.

"You have a visitor," Diana said when she'd finished, and Kiara's heart stopped. It simply stopped. Then pounded so hard she felt light-headed.

He had come. He was here.

She whirled around, her pulse a wild staccato in her throat, to see the speculative way Diana looked at her.

And then she would have given anything to take her reaction back, to hide it away, because her mother saw far too much and was always looking for more—but it was too late.

"It's only Harry," Diana said. Her brows arched. "I hope that's not a disappointment."

"Of course not," Kiara said with as much equanimity as she could muster. She couldn't quite smile. "Why would it be?"

Diana let her paper drop to the scarred surface of the old oak table, focusing in on her daughter with all of her sharp, incisive attention. Kiara steeled herself.

"I'm really not in the mood for an inquisition," she began, but sighed when she saw the look on her mother's face.

"Perhaps it's time to stop wandering about the chateau like a ghost," Diana suggested. Calmly. She was always so calm. It had the immediate effect of making Kiara feel wild and out of control. "Perhaps it's time to reclaim your career. Do more than simply mark time in your life."

"I'm fine," Kiara said. Insisted.

"Clearly," Diana said drily. She shook her head. "You claim there's nothing to discuss, that your marriage is in perfect health though here you sit, with no sign of your royal husband and as far as I know, no plans afoot to see him." She let that sit there for a moment. *"Perfectly fine*, as you say."

"I am not *marking time*," Kiara said, ignoring the rest of what Diana had said. "If you don't want me to stay here, I'm sure I can find a hotel nearby."

"If you want to stay in a hotel rather than in

your family's home," Diana replied in the same dry way, which somehow made it worse, "I won't stop you. Though I will, naturally, wonder why it is you would rather hide out in a hotel than face a few innocent and well-meaning questions about a marriage you claim is doing so well."

Kiara took a deep, hard pull of her coffee and wished, not for the first time, that she didn't always feel like this when Diana spoke to her— so torn between that sense of duty mixed with guilt, and that powerful yearning to feel neither.

"My marriage is fine," she said, fighting to keep her voice even. She wished she felt less shaky, the aftermath of that hard kick of misplaced adrenaline making her feel a bit sick to her stomach. "And still off-limits as a discussion topic."

She didn't know what her plan was, she realized as she heard her own voice, her own denials, flying around the kitchen as if she believed them herself. She'd asked Azrin for a separation and he'd, if not precisely agreed, let her go. It had been nearly a month so far, when they'd never gone longer than two weeks without seeing each other. Of course Diana had noticed. Was she simply going to brazen it out? Act as if nothing was wrong when another month slipped by, and then another? How long could she expect that to last realistically?

Why couldn't she admit what had happened? That she and Azrin had separated? Why couldn't she just *say* it?

"Here's what I can't help but notice," Diana said, far too calmly, instead of answering the question. "This is the most animated I've seen you since you arrived back home. Apparently being argumentative suits you. There's a bit of life in your eyes and color in your cheeks."

"This is not animation." Kiara felt something hot slide behind her eyes, and was appalled to think she might crack, might actually cry, right here in the kitchen. And she knew if she did, there would be no hiding the truth from Diana. She would have to tell her mother that the marriage she'd always opposed had failed. And she knew she simply couldn't do it. "This is a desperate bid for you to please, please stop poking at my marriage. I've been begging you to stop for five years!"

Diana gazed at her for a long, simmering sort

of moment and Kiara felt something turn over inside her. Hard. She just *knew*, somehow, that whatever her mother was about to say would take recovering from, and she wasn't sure she could recover from anything else just at the moment. She didn't think she could survive Diana's version of home truths. Not now. Not when she was terrified that she was, in fact, the very ghost Diana accused her of being.

"Listen—" she began, but then was saved when Harry Thompson walked in the door from the outside, keen to talk about the conversation he'd just had with the Frederick Winery chief winemaker.

Dear, friendly Harry, Kiara thought, studying him after they'd exchanged greetings.

She supposed he was a good-looking man, though it had been a long time since she'd thought of him in that way. He was simply Harry. He would one day run his family's wine business. He would raise a few children to follow in his footsteps. He would have good years and bad, as dependent as everyone else was on the vagaries of the Australian weather, the moisture in the soil, the odd heat wave or downpour that could change the year's grape yield. Safe, sweet, dependable Harry.

As Harry and Diana engaged in a friendly debate about their different winemakers' approaches to the Riesling this season, Kiara gripped her coffee and watched them over the brim of the mug.

The truth was, she could understand why Diana still thought Harry was the right choice for Kiara. He'd grown up steeped in wine and the wine business, and for a woman like Diana, who had lost her partner so early and had had to learn the wine business on the run with a small daughter and so many naysayers, he must look like the safest of safe bets. He must look a lot like Kiara imagined her own father must have looked to Diana all those years ago—a kind, loyal family man with deep roots in this valley.

It made Kiara wonder why she had let her romantic relationship with him fizzle, without even a harsh word spoken if she recalled it right, when she'd set off for university. Had she never really wanted *safe*, after all? Despite what she'd told herself before meeting Azrin?

"Are you expecting a big tour group?" Harry asked, stopping in the middle of his lively, friendly argument with Diana to peer out the big kitchen windows that looked out over a portion of the long entry lane leading up to the chateau and the grounds. It wound its way through the vineyards and beneath the small hill where the chateau sat, making the most of the view. "That's quite a convoy."

Kiara followed his gaze with mild interest, but saw nothing but dust kicked up in the air, as whatever vehicles Harry had seen had already disappeared around one of the bends, presumably circling around the final curves toward the front of the chateau.

"No tour group that I'm aware of," Diana said. "But I would be the last to know."

Kiara realized they were both looking at her. "I've no idea," she said. "I haven't given a tour of the winery since I was on my summer holidays from university."

Harry's face cracked into a big smile then, so warm and happy that Kiara found she was unable to do anything but smile back. There was some part of her that mourned the fact that he could never, would never, be the man for her. Surely, she thought, that spoke to defects in her character. Surely she should have wanted him—for all the reasons her mother wanted him for her.

Because if she married Harry or someone like him and lived her life out making wine here, she would be living out the very dream that Diana had wanted for herself—the dream that had been cut short and altered so terribly when Kiara's father died.

And Kiara couldn't help feeling that helpless guilt roll through her again, because she knew it would never happen. Not even if she never laid eyes on Azrin again. Not ever.

"Do you remember that summer right before you started university?" Harry was asking. He turned to Diana. "I don't know how you let us get away with it, to be honest." He launched into a tale of some childhood adventure Kiara had half forgotten.

She was laughing when the door to the outside opened again, as Harry reenacted his own teenage response to the trouble they'd got in. Assuming it was one of the many staff members, Kiara didn't even turn to look.

"That sounds like a delightful story," Azrin said in his coldest voice, the chill of it slicing through Kiara's laughter, straight into her heart, making her freeze solid and then whip around to take in the impossibility of him standing there, so fierce and hard and with that frigid gleam in his not quite blue eyes. Even so cold, so forbidding, he burned into her, making her momentarily blind. "I'm sorry to interrupt."

He was dressed entirely in black, which only served to make him that much more intimidating, something she would have thought impossible. A black T-shirt hugged his powerful torso and the black trousers he wore beneath did the same, and yet, despite the casual clothes, he was obviously and overpoweringly a king. He looked as regal as he did lethal, like some kind of dangerous angel, conjured up from who knew what kind of erotic dream to loom here, all smooth muscles, hard aristocratic stance, and implied danger. There was no mistaking that masculine threat, that ingrained assumption of dominance. It was written on every hard-packed inch of him.

He never took his gaze from Kiara. And yet that banked sensual menace, that unmistakable air of command, seemed to come off him in waves to blanket the whole of the room.

She could feel him in her bones, as if he had worked his way into the very marrow of her. And she could not seem to tell if what she felt so deep inside, that sweeping, twisting wave of sensation, was jubilation or despair.

Or both.

"Hello, Kiara," Azrin said in that dark, seductive way of his that set off fires inside of her, whole bright blazes she hadn't felt since she'd walked away from him in Washington and couldn't seem to breathe through now. There was only the lick of flames and that mad urge to throw herself directly into them. Into him. His mouth pulled into a crook that was not quite mocking, and yet was entirely too knowing. "My queen."

"Poor Harry," she said, her voice chiding.

It was the first thing she said to him, directly to him, and she didn't stop walking as she said it, she only ushered him into the sitting room on the family side of the chateau as if he was nothing but a guest. One she hardly knew, come to that. Azrin wasn't particularly impressed by that kind of reception from the woman whose absence had tortured him, flayed him alive, and in point of fact still did—but he shoved his own reaction aside.

This was all a means to an end, he told himself as he followed her. His desired end, whatever he had to do to achieve it. Whatever it took.

She turned back toward him once she'd walked all the way into the room, and it hit him then, the weight of the strain between them. It seemed to echo in the air between them, making its own noise. He couldn't help but drink her in, as if he'd been thirsty for her all this time.

He knew it was no more that the truth—he had been. He was.

She was dressed very casually in sand-colored trousers and a top that clung to her mouthwatering curves and was the precise shade of ripe cherries. Her light brown hair was pinned back from her face, but still fell to her shoulders in waves, and it caused him physical pain not to reach over and touch it. Her. He could not have said why he wanted her so terribly, so completely—but it had always been this way. She had always defied reason.

He had to order himself to keep from touching

her, little as his own body wanted to obey him. He wanted to drag her mouth to his and end this absurd distance between them. He wanted to take her down to the floor and remind her exactly how good it was between them—but too well did he remember what she'd said in Washington. Her accusations echoed in his ears even now, every bitter word like a separate knife into his gut. That all they had between them was that chemistry, that need.

"Harry who?" he asked, bored by what was obviously a stalling tactic.

"You know exactly who he is." She rolled her eyes. "And he didn't deserve the look you gave him."

Azrin smiled with a benevolence he did not feel, and somehow managed to keep his hands off of her as he lowered himself to lounge on one of the sofas. He barely glanced at the rest of the room, done with that brisk, efficient elegance that so categorized this place. These people. He propped his chin on one hand and eyed Kiara instead as she perched on a nearby chair, clearly determined to keep a safe distance between them. It irritated him beyond measure.

This was his wife. His queen. And she was afraid—or unwilling—to be too near him. He had to lock down the great surge of fury and something else far deeper, far darker, that moved in him then, threatening to take him over.

"I can assure you, Kiara," he said in a voice he could not quite control, "I saw only you."

Her gaze snapped to his for a moment before she looked away again. She moved her shoulders—as if she was bracing herself. As if she had to prepare herself to speak with him, as if she could no longer simply do it. He hated all of it.

"Looming about all menacingly in the kitchen and trying to intimidate everyone around you is not how we do things here," she said in some version of her usual teasing tone. This one, however, was laced through with something far sharper. "Though we certainly have names for it."

"I was not trying to intimidate anyone," he said mildly enough. Which was perhaps not in the least bit mild. "You would know it if I had been, I am certain."

She shook her head as if she despaired of him. He let his gaze travel all over her, and enjoyed it when she flushed. There was so much to say, to work through, and yet all he could seem to concentrate on was the simple satisfaction of being with her again. Of affecting her. Of making her react to him instead of simply walking away from him. He was sure that made him a fool, and he couldn't even bring himself to care.

"You look tired," he pointed out because he knew it would make her eyes narrow in outrage, and it did. "Sleepless nights? An unquiet mind, perhaps, interfering with your rest?"

"Not at all." She met his gaze then with the full force of hers, brown and deep and, he couldn't help but notice, shadowed. She angled her chin up in some kind of defiance. "I've never slept better."

Azrin didn't bother to call her a liar. He didn't have to. He could see the smudges of sleeplessness below her beautiful eyes, like twin bruises. He could see how pale she still was, though that did not seem to diminish either her prettiness or his automatic response to it. He found her as bewitching as ever—more, he acknowledged, because she seemed so unusually vulnerable.

And he was not above feeling it as a kind of victory that her return home had not resulted in an immediate return to her former vitality. That this separation was as terrible for her as it was for him. That she was not blooming into health and happiness without him. What would he have done if she was?

The air between them seemed to stretch, then tighten. Finally, she shifted in her seat, as if the tension was getting to her as much as it was to him. He had the impression it was hard for her to look at him again. Or perhaps he only wanted it to be. As if that might be telling.

"Why are you here?" she asked quietly, staring down at her hands as if they fascinated her suddenly.

"To discuss the terms of our separation, of course." Which was true, in its way. She flinched, then looked toward the open door. He watched her, his eyes narrowing in speculation. Was that guilt? His body thrummed with a kind of anticipation. "Is it a secret?"

"Not a secret, of course. But I haven't got around to telling anyone."

"Meaning it's a secret."

"Meaning I haven't got around to telling anyone," she repeated, frowning at him. "It doesn't mean anything more than that."

He studied her for a moment. "Why not?" When she frowned again, as if she didn't understand him, he sighed. "Why haven't you told anyone? I can understand not wishing to call a press conference, but surely this is precisely the news your mother has waited all these years to hear. Why would you deny her?"

She shook her head, her frown deepening. She pulled in a breath.

"I thought I knew who I was marrying," she said in a small voice. "What I was getting myself into. I thought I knew what I was doing." Her shoulders rose and then fell. "I was wrong."

He let that sit for a moment, ignoring the wild pounding inside of him that wanted only to reject her attempts to distance herself. Even in words.

"Let me understand you," he said coolly, when he could speak without any hint of temper. Or, worse, that shameful desperation. "Your intention is to simply slip back into your old life? Pretend none of this ever happened?"

The look in her eyes then hurt him.

"I doubt it would work," she said almost ruefully. "But what else can we do?"

"This is the solution you have come up with." It was not exactly a question, and her gaze became wary as she watched him. He leaned back against the sofa, the better to keep himself from reaching out to her. "This is the best you can do, after all of these weeks apart."

"I didn't say I was ready to discuss anything today," she pointed out crisply. "You chose to simply appear here without any warning. You can't possibly expect me to be anything but thrown off balance."

"You have not bothered to keep in touch, Kiara," he said, his hold on his control slipping again, and his temper bleeding through despite his best efforts. "What was I meant to do?"

"You were meant to give me space," she retorted. She shook her head, as if cataloguing all of his shortcomings, all of her complaints. "You seem to have a very hard time listening to the things I want and need, Azrin. It's difficult not to assume that speaks to deep and abiding flaws in our relationship."

"If I recall your comments in Washington correctly," he bit out, "and I am certain I do, there is not a single aspect of our relationship that you don't find flawed. Or did I misunderstand your suggestion that I take a second wife? And perhaps even a third?"

He did not imagine the way she stiffened then, the way her lips pressed tightly together.

"Are you here to tell me you've found a few good candidates?" she asked, and he did not imagine the edge in her voice, either. *Good*, he thought, a dark satisfaction running through him then. Why should he be the only one to take exception to that particular suggestion?

"Perhaps I should ask you the same question," he replied, suddenly far calmer than he'd been. "Wasn't that my supposed replacement I saw out in the kitchen?"

Kiara closed her eyes briefly, then opened them again. They were too bright, but she made no attempt to hide that from him, she only looked at him. He thought he saw the faintest tremor move over her lips, but she rubbed her hand over her jaw and he could not be sure.

"I don't want to do this," she said in a low voice. "I don't want to fight with you. It only proves how little we know each other after all this time, and it breaks my heart." She pulled in a breath. "We come from very different worlds, Azrin, just as everybody warned us. Our parents, the papers, angry strangers on the internet. Maybe we should end this now before we wind up hating each other. I have to think that would be even worse."

He moved then, leaning toward her but not quite closing the distance between them. As ever, he felt the burn of it. The fire, the connection. Her eyes widened, but she didn't shrink away from him. He was desperate enough to think that might be progress.

"What would it take?" he asked. "What do you think could fix this?"

She shrugged helplessly, a gesture of surrender that he found stuck into him like something sharp. He didn't want her to give in, this strong, stubborn woman. To give up. He wanted anything but that.

"I don't think we can, unless you have access to a time machine." She let out a small sound. "How else could we go back and really figure out who we are?"

"Do you think I don't know who you are, Kiara?" he asked, aware that his voice was little more than a rasp in the quiet room.

"I know you don't," she said, some of the hardness returning to her gaze, her mouth. But then she seemed to shake it off. "But the truth is, I thought you were someone else entirely. I knew a man who was only a prince as an aside. I was completely unprepared for what you'd become when you became a king."

"I am the same man," he said. His voice was too harsh, too sure. The words seemed to fall between them like stones.

"You are not." Her voice was firm. When her eyes met his, he saw the gleam of something he didn't fully understand and certainly didn't like.

This was worse, he thought then—worse even than gestures of defeat. This quiet, soft-spoken talk of the end of them, as if Kiara was conducting a pale, distant postmortem. The wildness was easier; the passion and the pain. The fight. This was intolerable.

"I think you misunderstand me," he managed to say in a voice somewhere near even. "In fact, I know you do."

"See?" She opened her hands wide. "You are making my point for me."

He had to move then and he did, rising from the sofa and somehow not going to her, not touching her, not showing her the vivid truth of them that he could feel arcing between them even now, even as she talked so resolutely about an ending he could not, would not accept. He prowled to the window and stared out, seeing nothing. No acres of vines, no blue sky above, no distant hills.

"What if we could make our own time machine of sorts?" he asked without turning around to face her. "You made a lot of claims in Washington. That I pushed you into dating me, into sleeping with me, into marrying me. What if we dated on your schedule instead?"

There was no sound at all for a beat, then another. Then she made a sort of scoffing noise. Azrin turned then. There was a hectic color splashed across her cheekbones that could as easily be temper or desire. Or some potent combination of both.

He raised his brows at her, daring her, and waited.

"What are you talking about?" she asked after another long moment. "That's ridiculous."

Her voice was cross. Annoyed. But he was sure there was something beneath it. He could feel it. He knew it—because she was wrong. He knew *her*.

"Why is it ridiculous?" he asked, finding to his surprise that he was suddenly able to project a great calm he did not feel. At all.

"We can't just pretend that nothing's happened between us!" she threw at him, her eyes wide, that color deepening in her cheeks. "That we're not married, that you're not...*you*. We can't *date!*"

"We don't have to pretend that we're not who we are—that would defeat the purpose." He spoke with such authority, as if he was not making this up on the spot.

As if this was not a last-ditch attempt to talk her into something he knew neither one of them would ever forgive him for simply taking. Though perhaps only he knew how close he was to doing so—simply throwing her over his shoulder like some kind of barbarian and to hell with what she said she wanted.

"We can pretend that we have just met," he

continued like a civilized man would. "You say I don't know you and I say that if that's true, we can fix it. Introduce yourself to me. Tell me who you are." He shrugged. "Perhaps you will find you don't know me as well as you think you do, either. Perhaps we will find there are whole worlds yet to discover between us."

She stared at him.

"You're serious," she breathed.

She swallowed, then shook her head as if she couldn't believe it. As if she doubted what she was seeing, hearing. Or perhaps she only wanted to doubt it.

"Come, now, Kiara," he said silkily. "What do you have to lose?"

CHAPTER SIX

SHE had everything to lose, Kiara thought some time later. But that wasn't something she could tell him, not without admitting how lost he made her feel, or how easily he could have made her stay with him in Washington, had he only pressed the issue.

They sat together out on the wide stone terrace that overlooked the gardens and the winery's busy cellar door, watching the summer tourists come in flocks and buses and even on foot to sample the Frederick wines and the food they served in the small, adjacent restaurant.

The day was impossibly perfect all around them, as if it was colluding with Kiara to show off the beauty of the valley to Azrin, to demand he take notice. They had debated Azrin's absurd idea in the sitting room for a long time, until Kiara had been sure her head was going to break into pieces, and they'd agreed, finally, to take a break from it. A small negotiated oasis of peace.

"Surely," Azrin had drawled in that sardonic way of his, "we are not so lost to each other that we cannot enjoy each other's company. If only for a little while."

There had been no particular reason for that remark to set her teeth on edge, and yet it had.

Nevertheless, Kiara had taken Azrin on a tour of the vineyards, showing him all the ways Frederick Winery had changed since he'd last been here for any serious length of time, back when they'd started dating. She couldn't pretend that there wasn't a huge part of her that was trying to prove something to him as she did it. *Look at the scale of our operation*, perhaps. *Pay attention to how I'm needed here, and why*, she'd said without using the words, with every single vine and barrel she'd pointed out to him.

Azrin, of course, had said nothing. He'd only watched and listened, had seemed to consider the things she'd showed him, with that intense focus of his that made her heart seem to work harder in her chest.

After the impromptu tour, they'd sat down for

a simple lunch full of local flavor that Kiara had pulled together from the usual reserves in the chateau's kitchen. She'd put thick slices of freshly baked bread, a few German sausages and a selection of local cheeses on a platter. Then she'd fished a bit of pear chutney from the pantry and, after a moment's thought, a particularly spicy beetroot relish, as well. She'd added small bowls of almonds and olives, and a dish of salted olive oil to dip the bread in.

Neither one of them wanted wine despite the fact there was so much of it available; a necessary precaution in her case, Kiara reasoned, given Azrin's historic ability to run roughshod right over her even without any wine involved.

Or was it more accurate to say it was usually *her* decision to give in to whatever it was he wanted, whether he asked her for her surrender or not? She wasn't sure she liked that thought, and concentrated on the food instead.

For a long time, they simply ate together at one of the small tables nestled there in the shade, in a silence she might have thought was peaceful, even companionable, had she not known better. Had the tension between them not added some kind of indefinable seasoning to each bite she took, a sort of prickle to the breeze that played over the table, even a certain heat to the measuring way his storm-tossed eyes moved over her when he thought she wasn't paying attention.

"You can't really want to walk away from our marriage without at least *trying* to fix it," he said after one such look in that darkly seductive way of his—breaking the silence and the peace between them that easily, though there was a part of Kiara that welcomed it the way she welcomed the onset of a storm after too long beneath threatening clouds. "That doesn't sound like the Kiara I know."

She decided she hated him for that. It explained the acrid taste in the back of her mouth, that unpleasant rolling sensation in her gut. *Hate.* Clearly.

"They will say you could not handle being queen," he continued, seemingly unperturbed. "There will be wild speculation. Is it because you secretly detest my people, my country, as we always suspect Westerners will? Or is it simply because you could not be expected to be sophisticated enough to handle the position, having come from what is, essentially, a glorified farming community?"

She had to bite back the sharp words that crowded her throat—and then she saw that almost silver gleam in his gaze, that slight curve of his hard mouth. *Of course.* He was pushing her. Deliberately.

"You are manipulating me," she said stiffly.

"I am *trying* to manipulate you," he corrected her, his voice suspiciously mild. Was he amused? That made her stomach twist. *Anger*, she told herself. *This is nothing more than anger.*

"Then you've lost your touch completely," she said. "If I cared what other people thought, I wouldn't have married you in the first place, would I? I doubt I would have so much as had that first dinner with you. I'd have been far too cowed by all the dire predictions about harems and compulsory burkhas."

Azrin only smiled, but, in spite of herself, she found herself thinking back to those wild, early days as she looked at him.

She'd fallen for him so hard and so fast that she'd spent months pretending otherwise out of simple fear. Terror, even. That he'd know. That he'd leave. She hadn't been able to decide which would be worse, which would hurt more. She hadn't wanted to find out.

It had been so intense—and so physical. A simple look from him and she'd turned to flame. A kiss, a brush of his fingers, being held against that hard body of his, and she'd detonated. It had been almost overwhelming when she'd realized—when she'd finally allowed herself to believe—that he felt the same way.

Meanwhile, everyone she knew had weighed in with their opinions. Everyone had known a great deal about the predatory nature of the average sheikh, apparently, despite none of them having known any sheikhs personally. She'd heard chapter and verse, again and again. And none of it had done anything at all except convince her that she knew better. That she knew *him*. That Azrin had been worth suffering through whatever silly fantasies her friends and family had wanted to concoct about him, simply because he hadn't grown up with grapevines wrapped around his limbs and a good Shiraz running in his veins.

She'd had so little doubt back then. She'd been so convinced she knew best. She'd been *sure*. Of

Azrin, of herself. Of them. When had she lost that? How had it happened? Did the fact that she'd let go of it so easily mean it was never there in the first place?

She shouldn't have been surprised at how sad it made her to think so.

"Are you reconsidering your position?" he asked then, as if he was able to see straight into her memories right along with her. "It's easy to say one cares little about public opinion, and harder, I find, to actually live through it."

"I've lived through it already," she pointed out quietly, as a flash of something bitter snaked through her as if it had been lying in wait, without her knowledge. "I'm living through it as we speak. The updates in the paper about the state of my royal womb, for example."

It was only after she said it, and Azrin only sat there with that expression on his face—as if she'd hauled off and slapped him with all of her strength, straight across the mouth—that Kiara acknowledged the possibility that she perhaps cared a bit more about public opinion than she wanted to admit. She jerked her gaze away from his, and only looked back when he reached over and took her hand in his. She observed, as if from a distance, that so simple a touch sent a jolt straight through her, searing her from neck to ankles.

She missed him. She stared at their joined hands and pretended that wasn't true, that it didn't beat in her like a drum. But she knew better. She missed him so much she made up wild fantasies of hating him to try to distract herself. Fooling no one, least of all herself.

"Do you still love me?" he asked.

His voice was quiet, but the simple question echoed through her as if he'd shouted it. She flinched as if he had. Still, she focused on their hands, not on his face. Not on those too-knowing eyes.

"I'm not sure that matters," she said, aware of how choked she sounded, of how that, in itself, undercut her attempt to shrug this away.

He only waited.

She heard the usual, familiar sounds of summer all around her. Rainbow lorikeets chattered in the trees above them, while the laughter of the kookaburras floated on the breeze. The tourists at the other tables on the terrace were laughing and talking, reveling in the shade and the sunny day all around them. She could smell fresh cut grass and oak barrels, the tang of grapes and the rich, fertile earth itself, the particular perfume that told her she was here and nowhere else. Home.

But that was not as comforting as it ought to have been. As she thought it should be.

Finally, unable to put it off any longer, unable to stand her own pathetic diversionary tactics, she looked at him.

It shouldn't hurt this much. He shouldn't feel like coming home, when he was anything but that. When he was the opposite of that, in fact, and well had she learned that lesson these past months.

"Do you?" he asked again, a certain implacable note in his low voice, a hint of his formidable will.

She let out a breath. Or it escaped. Either way, she knew he would not stop asking. That there was no hiding from him. From this.

"You know that I do," she whispered, knowing even as she said it that it was a kind of surrender. Or, perhaps, no more than a simple, overdue acceptance of a painful truth that somewhere along the way she'd decided didn't matter anyway.

He knew it, too. She saw the knowledge of it in his gaze, could feel the heat of it between their hands. She only wished she did not wonder if it was some kind of curse. Something they should have run *from*, all those years ago, rather than *toward*.

She supposed this was the time to find out, once and for all.

"I love you, too," Azrin said quietly, all of their history like a rich current pulsing between them, impossible to ignore, as his mouth moved into something not quite as simple as a smile. His hand tightened around hers. The curve of his mouth deepened. "So, Kiara, please. Date me."

"I can't help but notice that this is not Madrid," Kiara said drily.

They stood together out on the nondescript tarmac of what was little more than an airstrip. If she had not been looking out the window as Azrin's private plane had descended toward the shift and roll of the endless desert, she would have had no clue at all to tell her where they were.

There were no markings, not even on the faintly military-looking set of buildings off to one side.

The air was hot and shockingly dry, and yet she knew she was lucky it was still winter here; in the summer, in the desert, the temperature climbed so high it would have felt like a physical blow to step into it. The wind whipped into her, around her, and there was the faint sting of sand in it, making her wish she was wearing the headscarf she usually donned when she knew she would be arriving in Khatan.

She'd recognized the towering cliffs and the sea as they'd flown in, circling inland to land on this dusty little tarmac. She knew the picturesque village that was arrayed along one of the gentler cliffs, stretching down toward the pristine white sand beach beneath. She even knew that its name meant something like *beautiful dwelling place* in Arabic.

She should—she'd seen it featured on a thousand postcards in Arjat an-Nahr, and throughout the rest of the country.

Not that she'd ever been here before. Nor had she had any plans to change that.

"No," Azrin agreed, finally sliding his mobile

into his pocket. She couldn't see his eyes behind the dark sunglasses he wore, but she could feel the dark caress of them making her skin prickle. "We are not in Madrid."

He beckoned for her to proceed him as he started across the tarmac. Kiara started walking, noting the absence of the hand he usually held at the small of her back, and finding that she mourned its loss.

"I'm trying to figure out what part of our discussion, in which I clearly stated we should have our so-called first date in Madrid and you agreed, led you to think I instead wanted to come back to Khatan," she said, shoving the odd sense of some kind of grief aside. "Oddly, it's not coming to me."

"Did I agree?" he asked in that mild way that made her far too conscious of that ruthlessness he hid beneath his usually more accessible exterior. "Are you quite sure?"

Kiara opened her mouth to assert that he most certainly had, and then closed it.

She had been the one to talk about Madrid, in fact, once she'd agreed to this plan of his. It was a city they'd barely visited in all their crisscrossing of the globe. A blank canvas, she'd said, on which they could paint anything they liked as they played this little game. Privately, she'd thought it was the perfect choice—it lacked any markers of their complicated personal history, yet was big enough and not too remote, which meant that they could part without too much trouble should either of them wish it.

Should she wish it.

Yet all Azrin had said, now that she thought about it, was that Madrid was, indeed, a lovely city.

"You know I wanted to go to Madrid," she said, as if it was important. As if the city itself mattered, when she knew what truly bothered her was that he he'd made the decision without consulting her.

He looked down at her, and again she *felt* the look in his eyes even if she couldn't see it. She felt it move through her, making her whole body clench around the sensation. His hard mouth curved as if he could feel it, too.

None of this was fair.

"You agreed to the game, Kiara," he said, that heat in his voice seeming to stroke them both.

She didn't think that was fair, either. "I merely chose the venue."

They were respectfully handed into the second in a trio of kitted-out jeeps with four-wheel drive by Azrin's usual team of bodyguards, then driven over roads that seemed to Kiara like little more than suggestions or, perhaps, *intentions*, across the high, empty desert. Eventually, they made their way toward the cluster of palm trees and greenery that started at the very edge of the cliffs and then followed the often-photographed village down toward the gleaming sea beyond.

It took long, hard hours to drive across the desert to reach this particular stretch of coastline. There was no commercial airport—until today, Kiara would have said there was no airport at all. Travelers had to be hardy and determined to make their way here, but Kiara could see that it was well worth the trek.

The village boasted a collection of houses that seemed hewn from the cliff face itself, clustered very nearly on top of each other as they straddled the single road that wound through the town. There were two hotels next to each other steps from the bright white sand beach. The locals were reportedly friendly and welcoming, and those who made it here almost universally considered it the jewel of Khatan's mostly inaccessible and proudly inhospitable northern coast.

Kiara had read all about this place in the books she'd devoured while she and Azrin had been dating and then engaged, when she'd been so determined to soak up all the information she could about his country. About him. As if she'd expected there might be some kind of exam.

"I've always wanted to come to this village," she said now, remembering those long nights in her graduate school flat, reading about a place that seemed more fantasy than reality, all shining sun and gleaming sand, as the Melbourne winter had thrown rain and fog against her windows. "Though I did not imagine you would have to abduct me to make that happen."

Next to her in the backseat of the Jeep, Azrin merely shrugged. He had one hand braced against the door as the vehicle jolted down the rough cliff side road while he frowned down at the mobile that was once again in his other hand.

"You got on the plane of your own volition," he pointed out, that undercurrent of amusement making his dark voice rich in the confines of the Jeep. He didn't bother to look at her as he said it. He didn't have to.

Kiara rolled her eyes. She should be furious. She should feel betrayed, kidnapped, taken advantage of. But she was forced to admit to herself that she felt none of those things. What she felt was vulnerable. And she knew herself well enough to know that it didn't matter what corner of the world they might have gone to for this little game Azrin wanted to play. It was Azrin himself who made her feel so…at risk. So threatened.

And not by him but, far worse, by her own damned feelings.

She'd thought for some reason that a big, bustling city might dampen her reaction—might help dissipate the intensity of it—though she realized now that that had just been wishful thinking. When had the location made a bit of difference? It didn't matter if they were in Hong Kong or the Napa Valley. Azrin was like some kind of sorcery, and she was, apparently, helpless to resist him.

She could feel him, as usual, taking up too much space in the back of the Jeep. Dominating all of the air around him as well as the seat it-self. He even sat with that air of total command, his lean and powerful body seeming to infringe upon her, to take her over, without his having to move a muscle in her direction. And Kiara knew that it was all of this that she feared, all of this that made her feel so terribly weak.

It was not that he touched her, she knew; it was that she surrendered to that touch so completely. So totally. Without a single moment's hesitation or forethought. It was not that he demanded she forget everything that mattered to her when she looked at him; it was that she let herself forget it. She let herself fall.

She couldn't help but think that it was a terri-fyingly easy step from submitting to the sensual spell he wove with so little effort to surrendering to him totally—completely disappearing into him until she did nothing at all but smile politely and wait for him, forgetting that she had ever wanted more than that for herself. She'd felt that like a noose around her neck by the time they'd reached Washington—her own eradication happening all around her with every state dinner, every smile she aimed at a different dignitary she had to be so careful not to offend. What would be left of her? Anything at all?

Her mother had said as much before Kiara left.

"When will you be back?" Diana had asked from the door of Kiara's bedroom. Kiara had started, and then had wondered just how long her mother had been standing there. If she'd seen, for example, how emotional Kiara was valiantly attempting not to be.

"I'm not sure," she'd said, frowning down at the clothes she'd laid out before her as if it required fierce concentration to put together a small suitcase. As if, after all those years of constant travel, she couldn't do this sort of thing in her sleep. "I'll let you know as soon as I have a reasonable estimate, of course."

She had been speaking to her boss, not her mother. She'd been assuming that Diana had wanted that information so that she could continue to monitor Kiara's workload in her absence. She should have known better.

"Kiara…" Diana's voice had trailed away, uncharacteristically, and when Kiara had looked over at her, she'd been shocked to see a strange sort of expression on her mother's face. As if

Diana had been lost for words. Or simply lost. It had made Kiara feel knocked off balance. "You don't have to go with him. You don't have to do anything you don't want to do. You can stay here as long as you like. Stay a ghost, even. Until you work out whatever it is you need to work out."

There was a part of her that had yearned to accept that invitation—that had seen it as the olive branch it was undoubtedly meant to be. And it was even a good, short-term solution. Let Diana chase Azrin off while Kiara hid in her room like a child and licked her wounds. It certainly held great appeal. She'd already been doing it for a month.

But the rest of her had been far too wary of what it meant to give up control to Diana—and what Diana herself would have made of it if she did. Diana had never ceded control to anyone. Diana had created an empire out of sheer bloody-mindedness. Why couldn't Kiara do the same?

Not to mention, there was that stubborn core of her that couldn't bear Diana to think ill of Azrin, even by implication.

"Do you think so little of me that you think Azrin is bullying me into leaving with him?" she had asked, more sharply than was fair. "That I'm letting him?"

Guilt swamped her as soon as she said the words. She despaired of herself. It was easier to give in to her anger; it masked how truly conflicted she felt in her mother's presence and always had. But that didn't make it right.

"Of course not," Diana had said impatiently. "He's certainly an intimidating, formidable man, but you've never seemed remotely overwhelmed by it. I rather thought that was one of the things you liked about him."

"He's my husband," Kiara had said, fighting to keep her turbulent emotions under control. "I like a great many things about him."

Diana had sighed. "I was eighteen when I met your father," she'd said quietly. Too quietly. As if this was not the same old story she trotted out to reestablish their roles—to underscore her sacrifices and Kiara's failure to live up to them. "Only twenty when we had you. Before I met him I'd had all kinds of different dreams. I wanted to paint. I wanted a degree. I thought I'd travel. I had an enduring fantasy of running a bed-and-breakfast somewhere desperately remote, where

I could go weeks without seeing another living soul." She'd shifted where she stood, smiling slightly, as if at her own memories. "I'd never thought twice about wine. I don't think I could have picked out a vineyard if I'd been lost in one, much less the difference between the grapes. But I loved your father, and this was where he had to be, so this is where I came."

Kiara had stopped pretending that her clothes were so difficult to pack, that they'd required her full attention, and had turned to face her mother then, crossing her arms as she did it. As if she'd expected some kind of body blow. She'd never heard this before. She'd never heard Diana express anything even remotely approaching *regret*.

"It was hard," Diana had said softly, her much too similar brown eyes meeting Kiara's. "Much harder than I expected."

Kiara had shaken her head, refusing to give in to the confusing emotional storm that pounded through her then, making her question everything. Her mother. Herself.

Anger was easier. Safer.

"You've always said that the two of you were happy," she'd pointed out, fighting to keep that harsh edge from her voice. "Wildly happy, in fact."

"I'm not saying we weren't," Diana had countered. "I'm saying it was hard. More for me than for your father. He simply led the life he'd been raised to lead, while I had to learn how to be a part of it. But I still had my own dreams. Even after you were born. I thought I'd leave the winery to your father and pursue them on my own." She'd looked at Kiara for a long, uncomfortable moment. "But then he died."

Kiara had felt as if something had reached straight into her and had wrapped impossibly strong hands around her heart, her lungs, her stomach. And then had started to squeeze. She'd felt a surge of something she wanted to call fury, but it had been far too dark for that, far too edged with a deep current that felt too much like misery. And she'd refused to explore any of it. She'd understood with cold certainty that she didn't want to know.

"Let me see if I can parse this one out," she'd said instead, all of that anguish inside of her sharpening as she spoke, making her stand there like an ice sculpture and glare at Diana. "Either this is an anecdote about the perils of loving a man and moving with him into his predetermined life, or it's a rather more sentimental story about the need to follow my hopes and dreams despite my marriage. Which is it?"

As usual, Diana had seemed completely impervious to any show of temper. Or any insult. Also as usual, that had had the direct result of making Kiara feel like a toddler in midtantrum.

But that had been far preferable to what lay beneath. It always was.

"What I'm telling you is simple," Diana had said instead, with a little laugh that had sent Kiara's blood pressure skyrocketing. "After your father died, there were times that I looked around and wondered how on earth I'd ended up hip-deep in all of this wine when I'd never wanted anything to do with it. I'm lucky in that I've found that I'm quite good at it, but that's not always how this kind of story ends." She raised her elegant shoulders and then let them fall. "I know that becoming the Queen of Khatan is a role you took on as the price you had to pay to be with Azrin. I don't want you to look back on the choices you make now and find you regret them, Kiara."

She'd shrugged again, but there was something so sad about it that it made Kiara's throat seem to close. "That's all."

Kiara had felt a great wave swell in her then, and she'd been terrified it might be a sob, or the start of a great many sobs. It had rolled through her body and made her come much too close to shaking. Or worse. She'd hugged herself, hard, her fingers digging into her own flesh, and managed somehow to keep her eyes steady on Diana's.

"You make a lot of assumptions," she'd managed to say in a voice that was a good approximation of normal, even as it had been laced through with a lifetime of never feeling good enough for this woman, no matter what she did or didn't do. Of always falling short of Diana's endless sacrifices. And of the despair that lay like a thick pool beneath. "For all you know, the wine business was the price I had to pay to make you treat me like a daughter every once in a while, instead of just another employee."

Needless to say, Kiara thought now, staring broodingly out the window as the small convoy kept on moving past the pretty little village and along the barely perceptible trail that hugged the base of the towering cliffs, that exchange had not improved her relationship with her mother. It had only made her feel terrible about her own capacity for cruelty.

Kiara was forced to face the unflattering reality that she'd reacted as strongly as she had because Diana had managed, as ever, to push the hottest of Kiara's buttons. A simple story about losing her dreams in favor of her husband's, and Kiara had gone off like a rocket. Wasn't that why she'd left Azrin in Washington? Because she'd felt trapped, claustrophobic and muted in her new role? Because she'd been terrified that if she didn't leave, she would lose the will to try, and would be stuck forever in a position she hated, empty and useless, a figure standing always behind her husband with nothing of her own at all?

She felt the panic beat at her again, making her pulse race. She looked around the inside of the Jeep, taking in Azrin, the armed guards in front, the tinted windows that concealed them from the outside world. She should not have agreed to this foolishness. It was one more case of her thinking she could have her cake and eat it, too. She couldn't. She'd tried.

It didn't matter how much she loved Azrin, or how much he loved her. None of that changed anything. None of that even mattered, not really. None of that made him less a king, or made her any more suited to being the kind of queen he required.

She turned her head to tell him so, once and for all, and found him smiling a sweet, almost nostalgic smile. Not at her, she realized almost at once, even as her heart hitched in her chest. No, his gaze was directed out the window, at what looked to Kiara like a shadow in the great rock face that loomed above them.

As if he felt her gaze on him, he looked over at her, and Kiara felt something clutch inside her again. He looked…*carefree*, she thought, with some amazement. She couldn't remember the last time she'd seen such light in his fierce face, such uncomplicated joy.

It made her want to cry.

"This is my favorite part," he said, which didn't make any sense to her at all.

But before she could ask him what he meant,

the Jeep in front of them took what should have been an impossible, suicidal right turn. Directly into the cliff. Instead of smashing into rock, it disappeared as if it had been sucked straight into it, and Kiara only realized that the shadow was the entrance to a narrow canyon as their own Jeep took the same turn.

"Just wait," Azrin said calmly, as Kiara realized she must have gasped. "It gets better."

The narrow road twisted and zigzagged, hardly seeming wide enough for the Jeeps that very nearly scraped the jutting rock on either side as they performed a series of turns at speeds that indicated they were very familiar with this route. Or completely insane. Kiara craned her head around to look up, to see that there was only a faint ribbon of sky visible far above, the sheer walls of the canyon almost closing them in.

She should have felt trapped. Perhaps she did. She took a breath, then another, and still they drove on, heading deeper into the rocks, into what was surely the heart of the cliffs themselves. Were they headed underground? Into some kind of bunker? Did he want to attempt to *date* her, as he put it, in some kind of medieval Khatanian jail?

They drove on and on. It was gloomy this far inside the rocky cliffs, this far away from that sliver of sunlight far above them—gloomy and cold. And still they drove, the mountain seeming to loom all around them, the road they followed hardly deserving of the name.

"Azrin…" she began when she couldn't take it another moment, when she thought the immensity of the rock, its implacable weight and the relentless chill on all sides, might actually send her into a panic from which she'd never recover.

He reached over and took her hand, taking it to his mouth for a kiss that seemed, she registered, almost absent, even if the touch of his lips slid through her like the brush of velvet across her skin. He kept his eyes trained ahead, and after a long moment, then another, he smiled.

"It's only scary the first time," he told her, that indulgent tone too buoyant with that same joyfulness for it to grate, and then he nodded toward the window. "Because every other time, you know that the ride is worth it."

Kiara frowned at him, but she turned as he'd directed her, and lost her breath all over again.

Because on the other side of the window, spreading out before her as the tiny canyon widened and sunlight poured down from above, was paradise.

The narrow little canyon opened up into a wide gorge, where palm trees and other vegetation clustered and beckoned over a series of inexpressibly beautiful aquamarine pools. The glorious waters seemed lit from within, as well as from the sunlight pouring down from high above. Here, inside the protected valley, the sun warmed the rocks—the forbidding chill of the narrow approach an immediate distant memory.

Kiara hardly knew where to look first, and found herself sitting up and leaning forward like an overawed child.

The pools lay in a straight line along the floor of the canyon, each one larger than the one before it, seeming to dead-end at what appeared to be the farthest reach of the great hidden valley. And that was when Kiara actually let out a gasp, amazed. What could only be some kind of palace seemed to hang in the very air, as if carved from the rock itself, a five-story fortress garnished with balustrades and terraces, balconies and delicate arches, all of it jutting out over the water of the farthest, largest pool as if it had sprung full-grown from the side of the mountain.

As if it had always been there.

"It is called the Palace of the Ten Pools," Azrin told her, pride and a kind of reverence in his voice. "It was considered a holy place for many ages, and then became the favored summer retreat of my great-grandfather. Very few know of it."

"It's beautiful," Kiara whispered, though she could hardly speak past the sudden lump in her throat.

It was more than beautiful. The impossible, nearly belligerent thrust of the palace out from the rock cliff made her chest feel tight. It was a fierce, implacable building that shouldn't exist. It called to mind some warrior's mixture of gingerbread houses and medieval keeps, all jumbled together into what looked like a series of vertical rock sculptures, piled haphazardly on the side of a dizzyingly sheer cliff.

Azrin turned toward her, smiling, and it was

like sensory overload. She couldn't tell what her body was doing, what she wanted, she could only tell that it was *too much*. A secret palace, mysterious pools inside a mountain…how was she supposed to resist something like this? How was she meant to truly analyze what had become of them, of their marriage, if every time she turned her head, the beauty of their surroundings made her want to weep?

If he did?

"It hardly seems smart, though," she pointed out. She sat back and eyed him critically. "Bringing out your big guns so early on."

"Afraid you can't handle it?" he asked, that teasing light in his gaze.

He appeared perfectly at ease, lounging back against the seat as if he hadn't a care in the world as the Jeep brought them closer and closer to the impossible rock palace that some part of her still whispered couldn't possibly be real.

"I can handle it," she assured him. She waved her hand, encompassing the beauty of the pools, the fall of sunlight that seemed to bounce off the mountainsides, the dreamlike palace itself. "But what are you going to do for a second date?"

CHAPTER SEVEN

HE WAITED for her out on the highest of the wide balconies as the afternoon edged toward evening. Up above, the sky was beginning to ease into a darker blue, and the skeleton staff they'd brought along to run the palace had already lit all the lights that hung like lanterns around the stone and iron perimeter.

Azrin never tired of this place. Of the mysterious echoes against the rocks. Of the way he seemed able to breathe deeper here, the air clear and sweet. Of the enchanted pools themselves, so deep and beautiful, no matter the season. They soothed him, even when he did no more than gaze upon them. He'd swum in them as a child, sat beside them as an adult, allowed them to work their quiet magic on his soul.

Tonight they made him believe that all of this would work out precisely the way he wanted it to work out. The way it should.

The way it must, he thought, and pretended he did not notice his own urgency.

He sensed her before he heard the faint scuff of her foot against the stone, and turned as she walked out onto the balcony, and then, after the slightest, barely perceptible hesitation, toward him. He leaned back against the high iron rail and watched her approach.

His wife. His queen.

Kiara wore a flowing magenta tunic over loose fitting trousers, and only thin sandals on her feet. She had a wrap over her shoulders, in deference to the mild winter evening that was already cooling the air around them. Her hair swung free in loose waves that his fingers itched to touch, and when she drifted closer he saw she wore only minimal cosmetics, letting her natural beauty shine forth. Captivating him as he was sure she intended.

Or perhaps, he thought ruefully, she simply captivated him as she always had, no intention necessary.

He made no move to reach for her as she walked to the railing and stood next to him but not quite touching him, not quite allowing her thigh to brush against his. She gazed out over the rail at the hidden gorge spread out before them. He made no move at all, and it nearly killed him.

"I count only five pools," she said after a moment, her voice soft. Almost shy, he would have said, though that didn't make any sense at all. "Shouldn't there be ten?"

"There are ten."

She looked at him, her brows raised in query, and he smiled, awash in the simple pleasure of looking at her when she was not frowning back at him, not obviously sad or distant, her eyes that clear, gorgeous brown he'd loved for so long now and not filled with the anguish that he, somehow, always seemed to put there despite his own best intentions.

"There are two pools in a cave deeper inside the mountain," he said, nodding toward the sheer cliff that faced him and stretched up toward the desert floor far above them. "They are fed by a hot spring and are accessible only from the second level of the palace." He waved a hand to his left. "If you were to swim down beneath the waterfall at the end of this pool, you could access the small passage that leads to three further pools. Two small ones that have only rocks and towering cliffs and one that is really more properly a lake, complete with a small, rocky beach." He wanted to lean in closer. He wanted to capture her face in his hands and taste that wide, compelling mouth. He did neither, and he wasn't at all certain where the strength for that came from. "In total, ten pools."

She looked away again, and he watched the way her hands clenched at her sides, as if she fought off her demons even as she stood there, looking otherwise relaxed. He understood then that it was a great talent of hers—one he should have recognized as the warning it was much earlier.

"It doesn't seem real here," she said in that same soft voice, with that same curious reticence. "It feels as if a place like this shouldn't exist."

He gave in to his urges and reached over then, pulling a strand of her brown-and-gold hair between his fingers, feeling the raw silk of it against his skin. She smelled of citrus and spice, a kind of delicate perfume that was only hers, and he knew that whatever she thought was happening here, whatever she believed this game might prove between them, that he would never, could never let her go. He didn't have it in him. She had always been the one thing he was wholly, unrepentantly selfish about, his one weakness, and he didn't imagine that anything could change that simple fact.

No matter how distant they had become these last months. No matter what.

He supposed that made him as manipulative as she'd accused him of being, after all, and he couldn't bring himself to regret that as he should have done. As a better man would have done, he was sure.

"Are we already on our date?" she asked, her voice a shade or two too husky. But at least that hint of shyness was gone. At least she sounded like herself. "If so, you should know that it's incredibly forward to just grab someone's hair when you hardly know them. In some cultures that could get you killed."

"Lucky, then, that I'm the king of this one."

He gestured toward the small seating area arranged behind them, jutting out from the wall of the palace. There was a construction of canopies above to shield them from the sun by day and thick, heavy rugs to take the chill from the stones beneath them now, like some majestic, luxurious cabana. Large, colorful pillows were scattered about the floor, circling a wide, low table of inlaid mosaic tiles in shades of blue, green and black.

Azrin watched as Kiara lowered herself to the pillows with that absentminded, matter-of-fact grace of hers that he found so intoxicating. He threw himself down on the other side, unable to take his eyes from her pretty face. She tucked her hair behind her ears in a gesture that betrayed her nervousness, he thought—with a certain satisfaction that he could still affect her. That he still got under her skin.

If he was the better man he thought he should have been, he might have had some compunction about enjoying that. But he did not.

"We should lay down some rules," she said, her gaze touching his, then skittering away. "Before we begin this dating experiment of yours."

"You think we need rules?" He could think of other things they needed, none of which were appropriate for the moment. But they moved in him like heat. Like something narcotic, straight into the bloodstream.

"I do." Her brows rose again, but this time in something far more mocking, far less nervous. This was the Kiara he recognized. "Particularly if you are going to lounge about like that, like some kind of dissolute pasha."

He vastly preferred her like this, he thought. Despite any marks that sharp mouth of hers might leave on his skin.

"Were Khatan still under the rule of the Ottoman Empire," he drawled, "I would indeed be a pasha, as many of my ancestors were before me."

He eyed her across the table. She returned his gaze for a long moment, and he saw faint color spread across her cheekbones. He saw the way she swallowed, long and hard. He wondered for a moment if she would crumble, what it might mean if she did, but her eyes remained clear.

"Noted," she said quietly. "Rule number one— no flippant references." She sighed. "And we'll have to talk about sex, of course."

"This is the best date I've ever been on," he replied with silken delight, only partially feigned for effect. "Is that an invitation? My answer is an enthusiastic yes, of course."

"I don't think we should have any," she said primly, as if he hadn't spoken.

"This feels like déjà vu, Kiara." He felt that dark amusement ignite within him. "We might as well be in Melbourne five years ago. You will put up a token protest, we will fall into bed anyway, and you will marry me all over again. I had no idea we could sort all of this out so easily."

"I'm serious," she said, and he could hear the chill in her voice. The defensiveness. It kindled his banked temper into a bright blaze in an instant, fierce and hot. He slammed it back down as best he could.

"Of course you don't want to have any sex." He leaned back against the pillows and regarded her evenly. "You think that I use your body against you, confuse you with our sexual chemistry, control you somehow with it, whatever." He let that sit there for a moment, then raised a brow, daring her. "Isn't that right?"

"Speaking of flippant references," she said, her voice sounding faintly strangled. The color had deepened across her cheeks, making her seem to glow with the strength of her feelings.

"As a matter of fact," he said, "*I* don't think we should have any, either."

"You don't." Her voice was patently disbelieving. As if he was a wild animal instead of the man—*the husband*—who loved her to a distraction five years and incalculable complications into this marriage. It was infuriating. *She* was infuriating.

"I don't," he said, his voice hardening as he spoke, "because I grow tired of the way I am painted in this fantasy you have of our marriage. I think your sexual appetite is as voracious and encompassing as mine, which you used to admit freely. Revel in, even. But it does not suit you to think of it in those terms any longer. You prefer to be the victim, for reasons I'm sure you'd prefer I not speculate about."

"I don't want to be a victim!" Her voice was some mixture of shock and fury, and she sat up straighter, her eyes blazing across the table at him. "I'm not one!"

"You use sex as a weapon, Kiara," Azrin said matter-of-factly, propping himself up on an elbow to level a look at her. Her cheeks were wild with color now, and there was a hectic sort of look in her eyes, nearly black now with emotion. Or the burn of her temper. He was happy enough with either, whatever that might make him. "You claim it's all we have when the truth is, you make sure it's all we *can* have. I think it makes you feel safer. More in control."

"You use sex in place of conversation, in place of emotion, in place of what should be a real, healthy relationship!" she hurled back at him. There was no doubt she was furious—the air crackled with it, and Azrin thought that now, maybe, they could get somewhere. Now that her mask was off, that polite veneer tossed aside. "You never asked me how I felt about any of the changes that you threw at me—that were thrown at both of us—you just demanded I do as you said and then acted as if sex would fix the rest of it!"

"Then we agree," he said smoothly, tamping down his own temper, telling himself that this was neither the place nor the time. It was the rawness of what they still felt that had to matter, not all the analysis of what they'd each done to the other. It had to matter, he thought, or nothing did, and *that* was something he refused to accept. "No sex, unless it is a gift. Unless it is honest. No hiding from unpleasant truths or uncomfortable realities. And no wielding it as a weapon designed to make the other the villain."

"This is ridiculous," she snapped. "You might as well simply claim that up is down and day is night."

"Have you any other rules, Kiara?" he asked, hearing the edge in his voice despite his best efforts to soften it. "Any other reasons to drag this out?" He stared at her coolly. "It tempts me to wonder if you don't really want to get to know me, after all, as we agreed. It might contradict all these stories you tell yourself."

She jerked her gaze away from his, and there was nothing but silence for a long while.

Azrin watched her. He listened to the sounds of the pools all around them—the water lapping against the rocks, the splashing of the waterfall, the breeze that moved through the palm trees and made them rustle as if they, too, were restless. She was breathing too hard, too fast, her gaze directed straight down into her lap, and he suspected that if he could see her hands beneath the table they would be clenched into fists.

The shadows had lengthened into full dusk by the time she looked at him again, her brown eyes clear once more. Too clear, perhaps. She shifted where she sat, pulling her wrap tighter around her shoulders and smoothing it over her arms. She even smiled, for all that it was one of her meaningless, well-practiced political smiles.

He didn't let it get beneath his skin. Not tonight. He was happy enough to see a smile, any smile—and more than happy to take up the challenge that it entailed.

"So tell me," she said, her voice light, easy.

A sharp-edged mockery of first-date conversation, and well did he know it. And enjoy it. She propped her chin up with her hands as she leaned her elbows on the table, and gazed at him with an attention that bordered on the fatuous and almost made him laugh.

"Do you come here often?" she asked.

Game on, my love, he thought, and began.

"I've already told you what I do," Azrin said politely. So politely.

His voice was intelligent and amused, deep and

dark and sexy, and seemed to smooth its way down her spine and then wrap around into the very core of her. She'd always been entirely too susceptible to that voice. Hadn't that been one of the reasons she'd sat down at that café table in Melbourne? Any sane person would have walked away, or so she'd often told herself.

"You are the king," she said, as if reminding them both. Or herself, anyway. "Lord of all you survey, et cetera. That must be fun. Smiting your enemies, plundering and pillaging." She waited for his brows to arch in protest and smiled. "Figuratively speaking, of course."

"It is not fun at all," he said, his voice lower, then. More serious, suddenly, though he smiled slightly, as if to conceal it. "It is many things, and often rewarding, but no. There is nothing *fun* about it."

He glanced over his shoulder toward the palace then and waved a peremptory hand in the air. Kiara sat back and watched as his staff poured out from the nearby, arched entrance at that regal command, bearing trays piled high with all kinds of Khatanian delicacies.

There were dishes of rice, platters of grilled fish and a selection of carved meats. Delicate, flaky pastries that Kiara knew would be filled with combinations of meats and cheeses, spices and sugar. There was a plate of the most tender lamb, sliced open to show that it was stuffed with rice, eggs and onions, and was temptingly fragrant with the unusual combination of spices that Kiara knew to be traditionally Khatanian.

There were tall drinks of thick yogurt that would be flavored with cardamom or pistachio, and would perfectly complement the savory flavors of the rest of the food served. There were dishes filled to near overflowing with the ubiquitous dates and olives and almonds that grew everywhere, handmade hummus and tabbouleh, and plates piled high with the special Khatanian flatbread that shared characteristics with a Mediterranean pita or an Indian naan but was better than either, whether it was plain, roasted with garlic and olive oil, or stuffed full of coconut and dried fruit.

Kiara's mouth watered.

"Come on now," she said when his staff had bowed their way back indoors, leaving them to an expertly prepared feast to eat surrounded by candles and lanterns and the clear night sky above them, in the most magical place she'd ever seen. Or even dreamed. "You have to think some of this is fun."

Azrin only shot her a dark look she couldn't quite read as he reached for the flatbread and tore himself a thick piece.

"Feasts delivered at your command," she continued. "Jetting about the globe in a private plane. Palaces scattered about several countries, yours to occupy at will. This is the third one I know about in Khatan alone. And when I met you in Melbourne you drove that Ferrari and I know you thought *that* was fun."

She'd thought it was fun too, though she hardly let herself think about things like that any longer. She'd been so determined to think only about the difficulties, the impossibilities. The expectations and demands. The agony of all of this.

But beneath all of that, she still remembered the way the sleek, luxury car had hugged the famous curves along the Great Ocean Road. She remembered how Azrin had held one hand on the steering wheel and one resting high on her thigh, and how close she'd felt to flying there, the limestone cliffs on one side and the aching beauty of the sea against the rocks on the other.

She'd had the notion that she was as close to really flying free as she would ever get with this breathtakingly beautiful man, in such a heart-stoppingly perfect machine, on the very edge of the world. *Together*, she'd thought then, and it had felt as if they were truly soaring, the powerful car racing beneath them, as smooth and as sexy as he was and yes, fun.

When was the last time she'd thought about fun?

"You are talking about the privileges of wealth," Azrin said after a moment. He reached forward to dip his bread in the hummus. "That is not the same thing as being a king."

"Isn't it?" She was skeptical.

And she had to remind herself to breathe again, her heart racing as if she was still in that car, five whole years and half the world away on the prettiest road she knew, falling head over heels in love with the man who'd driven them with such easy grace and careless competence. She had to shake her head slightly to remind herself where she was, and more than that, *when*.

"There are a great many wealthy men who are responsible to no one but themselves," Azrin pointed out. "That is not an option when you have a country to run and would prefer not to run it into the ground."

His eyes narrowed slightly, as if he could see how far away she was, and where she'd gone. Which, she told herself sharply, he certainly could not.

"So what you notice most about your throne is the weight of it," she said, focusing back on this conversation, and not the phantom weight and heat of his elegant hand holding her against her seat so many years ago now, both promise and sensual threat. "Not the bowing and scraping. Not the fact that your every word is both command and law. Not the great good fortune of having access to all that wealth, that kingdom, the palaces that go along with it."

"What makes you think all of that is not, in itself, the weight I mean?" he asked softly.

Kiara didn't like the way that question resonated inside her, and directed her attention to the food instead, ignoring the small voice within that whispered she was little more than a coward.

That she didn't want to know any more than she already did—that what she knew already was too much and would take too much getting over as it was.

She started with forkfuls of a fish she couldn't identify, grilled to perfection with the tang of lime and deeper, more complex flavors beneath. She closed her eyes for a moment, savoring it.

"And you?" he asked. She opened her eyes to find him regarding her with heat in his gaze, kicking up an answering fire inside her. His mouth crooked. "What is it you do?"

"I'm a winemaker," she said.

She heard the way she said it, with that undercurrent of something very near belligerence, and saw that he heard it, too. But he only looked at her. She felt herself flush, and was unsure if it was from some kind of embarrassment or something else, something more closely tied to that molten heat that moved in her simply because he was near, no matter how she wanted to deny it.

"How did you become a winemaker?" he asked.

As anyone on a date would, she supposed. There was no reason it should have agitated her the way it did, like a splinter into flesh.

"It's the family business," she said automatically, shifting against the pillows. "I grew up on a vineyard." She let out a sigh as that impossible heat and everything else inside her seemed overwhelming suddenly—or was it that she felt too exposed? "This feels silly, Azrin. You know all of this. I know all of this. Nothing we're going to say tonight is going to change the fact that you want things I can't give you."

She had the impression he sighed, too, though she couldn't hear it over the sound of the white noise in her head.

"You have been my wife for five years," he pointed out, his voice even. "It only became too onerous for you, apparently, in the past four months. Why are you so certain those four months outweigh the previous five years altogether? I'm not sure I agree with that assessment." He shook his head when she started to speak. "But this is hardly appropriate first date conversation, Kiara. Don't force me to conclude that you want to sabotage this experiment before we even start."

She fumed. There was no other word for it. She stared at her plate for a moment and ordered herself to be calm. To breathe. She avoided looking at him for long moments as she loaded up her plate again. Fragrant rice, neither too soft nor too sticky. Perfectly cooked lamb with so many flavors packed into it. Tangy, rich olives, creamy hummus, and her favorite flatbread with garlic.

It was all so tempting, but she couldn't bring herself to take another bite.

"So what are you looking for in a queen?" she asked, instead of all the things she wanted to say, all of which seemed to crowd her throat. "If that's the kind of thing kings like to talk about on first dates. With perfect strangers like me."

His eyes gleamed silver, as if he found her amusing or possibly edible, and she had to repress a shiver of automatic reaction to either possibility.

"I like wine," he said, his mouth curving.

"Congratulations," Kiara replied crisply, refusing to find that comment endearing on any level. Damn him. "If that is your only criteria, you should have no trouble finding the perfect queen. You need only click your fingers and a queue will appear before you, wineglasses at the ready."

"You are right, of course."

He drew up one knee and leaned his arm against it. He could not have looked more like what he was—a mysterious desert sheikh, king of everything around them and for miles in all directions—if he'd tried. Perhaps he had tried.

He was dressed in the loose linen trousers he favored in private and a short-sleeved, buttoned shirt in the same whisper-soft fabric, both in shades of deep cream that made his olive skin seem that much darker, his long body that much more sleekly muscled. He looked cool, confident. Power seemed to emanate from him like heat, as if even his own casual clothes did not dare attempt to contain him.

Kiara found her throat was dry.

"My queen will be a symbol," he said after a moment. "Whether she wants to be or not. She must acknowledge the traditional values of my country, yet infuse her role with her own modern flair, her own achievements and strength. I want both and I would not be happy with anything or anyone less."

"And what if this…*infusion* can't exist?" Kiara asked, her voice harsher than it should have been, than she wanted it to be. "What if real women cannot be symbols, only imperfect spouses, and your lofty expectations will crush her where she stands?"

"My queen must be strong," Azrin said, his voice as quiet as his eyes were intent on hers. His voice seemed to ring in her, through her.

"Strong enough to be rendered completely silent?" Kiara countered. "Strong enough to be marginalized and forgotten, shoved aside, unable to complain or even comment on what is happening to her for fear she will be told she is *but one more fire* her king—not her husband—must put out?"

"Strong enough to know that none of those things are happening, even if it feels as if they are in a time of such confusion, right as her husband takes the throne," he retorted, his voice even, his gaze hot. Direct. Nothing so simple as anger there, she thought almost helplessly, but something deeper, far more raw. It made goose flesh rise over her arms, the back of her neck. "Strong enough to wait. Strong enough to keep from running."

"Most women are not psychic, Azrin," Kiara told him, her voice low and shaking with all the things she was trying so hard not to say. Not to scream. "They cannot divine intention from the ether, only from behavior. From what you say and how you treat them, in fact. And then act accordingly."

"Some women, upon marrying the crown prince to a kingdom, would not be quite so surprised when he became a king," Azrin said, his voice deliberately slow, as if she might have trouble understanding him. Trying to provoke her, she was sure, and seethed. "It is in the job description, after all. It's right there in the title, the kingdom. The simple fact of who I am."

"While some princes, upon marrying a woman not from their culture, might make it clear what their expectations are *before* there is any risk of ascending a throne."

"You make it sound as if you were chained to my ankle and dragged along in my wake," Azrin snapped then, his control clearly deserting him, which Kiara should not have felt like some kind of victory.

Hadn't she watched him really lose control in Washington—and hated it? What was the matter with her? She felt as if some great wave was rising in her, about to crest, but she had no idea what it was. She didn't *want* to know.

"I don't recall all this torture and torment, Kiara. When was this great silencing? Did I ask it of you or did you decide it all on your own? All I asked was that you support me. Was that really too much for you?"

"I don't want to be your mother!" she cried, the words ripped from somewhere inside her. The wave crashed into her, over her. The words she hadn't known she meant to say seemed to echo back from the night sky, the rock walls, even the pools. She lifted her hands in the air and then dropped them back down to the table. "I'm sorry, but I don't. It's as if she exists only as a projection of your father. A painting of his, maybe. A shadow. I don't want to be like that. Or like your sisters." She shook her head. "I won't."

"Nor do you seem particularly interested in being your own mother." He leaned forward then, and his dark eyes pinned her to her seat, made her feel paralyzed. And he knew it. She knew he did. "Yet isn't that exactly what you're doing? Choosing that vineyard above all else, and damn the consequences? Damn me, damn our marriage—when you don't even really know that it's what you want, after all?"

"Of course it's what I want!" But she felt breathless, suddenly, as if she'd run a race, and with that churning in her stomach, too, as if she'd lost. By miles. "It's what I've always wanted!"

Yet even as she said it she remembered what she'd said to her mother in her old bedroom in the chateau—what she'd all but hurled at Diana's head. And she couldn't help wondering if it was possible that Azrin knew things about her that she didn't, however much she wanted to deny that he could. Did he see the things she'd always been too afraid to say before? Did he know, somehow, exactly what she'd said to Diana? *Maybe the wine business was the price I had to pay to make you treat me like a daughter every once in a while.*

But she hadn't meant any of that, had she? She'd only wanted to strike out, strike back, at her mother. She'd only wanted to make a point. An unkind one, perhaps, but that didn't make what she'd said *true.*

Of course she hadn't meant it. Not really.

Azrin's gaze was pitiless then. And still so uncomfortably direct, seeing deep into her. Far too deep. Seeing things she would have sworn weren't there. *Because they aren't there*, she told herself fiercely.

She watched, holding her breath now, as an expression she didn't recognize moved over his face. Something she might have called sadness, had that made any kind of sense. As if he grieved for something, and she was suddenly much too afraid to ask herself what that could be.

He ran a hand over his face as if he was tired. When he looked at her again, his eyes were almost kind. And she thought he might have shattered her heart, just like that.

"Is it really what you've always wanted?" he asked quietly. "Are you sure?"

CHAPTER EIGHT

KIARA barely slept.

At a certain point, tired of turning this way and that without end, the fine linen sheets wrapped around her like instruments of torture, she'd stopped trying.

She'd half expected Azrin to appear with the dawn to start in with his particular brand of torment all over again. She'd braced herself for it, scowling hollow-eyed and sleepless at the gently billowing canopy that hung above her until the light outside her windows was the blue of just before dawn and she'd finally fallen into an exhausted, restless sort of doze.

But he didn't come. Not when her attendant brought her a steaming cup of strong, dark Khatanian coffee to herald the start of the new day. Not as the morning wore on, the sun streaming in the old windows, lighting up the oddly shaped chamber with its one wall of wholly unfinished rock, the rest seeming to simply hang from the mountainside, old woods and fine tapestries scattered here and there and thick, colorful rugs stretched over the smooth floors.

The night had ended abruptly. She'd simply stood up and walked away without another word, leaving him at the table without so much as a backward glance. She told herself now that it had been necessary—that once again, she'd needed space. From him. From the things he made her think about. Both.

"Until tomorrow, then," he'd murmured, the dark irony in his low voice following her as she'd retreated, yet another fresh hell to add to her collection.

Kiara told herself she was thrilled that he was otherwise occupied today. Delighted, in fact. She could lounge about this lovely, sun-drenched suite of rooms she'd been given, stuff herself with figs and almonds and sweet dates drenched in honey, and not spend a moment turning over everything that had been said the night before in her head.

But that, of course, proved impossible.

She found her way outside, onto the small, private balcony off her suite. She welcomed the day's warmth in the stones beneath her bare feet, a simple pleasure that felt more healing, perhaps, than she wanted to admit. She couldn't help but sigh as she looked out over the series of pools, a breathtaking view down the canyon that had grown no less stunning, even if she knew to expect it this time. She rested her hands on top of the sun-baked iron railing, and let the light from high above dance over her face.

And admitted to herself that she had never felt so lost. So alone. And empty, too—as if she'd been hollowed out, as if she was no more than a shell erected around all the things she'd held to be true, all the beliefs she'd had about herself. Her whole life and all she'd worked for. Her goals, her dreams. Azrin and this marriage of theirs. Even the past few months.

Did she use sex as a weapon, as he'd claimed? Did she really not know what she wanted from her life? Was she truly as uninterested in being like Diana as she was in becoming Queen Madihah, and if so, what did that mean?

The questions seemed to thud through her like heavy stones, one after the next.

Azrin was a forceful, commanding man. He

had been groomed since birth to lead. To be the king of this country and all that entailed. To rule. He was dark sometimes, even brooding. He had a temper, certainly. He was fierce. Demanding. Arrogant and ruthless. What he wanted he took, he'd told her once, and she knew it was true. She'd experienced it personally. But he was more than all of that—there was that flashing intelligence, that dry wit. His intense, shattering sensuality. His strong sense of duty. His kindness. He was a complicated man, by any reckoning. On some level, still a mystery to her.

But she had never known him to be anything but honest.

She didn't want to think about what that must mean. There were so very many things, she realized then, that she didn't want to think about. That she went out of her way to keep from thinking about, in fact. Not that it worked. Not entirely.

Strong enough to wait. Strong enough to keep from running.

That was what he'd said he wanted from his queen. From her. But she hadn't given him that, had she? She hadn't waited. She hadn't even attempted to give him the benefit of the doubt. She'd left on the very first morning she could without causing an international scandal, right after their official tour was finished. She'd run, despite the fact she'd always believed herself to be the kind of person who would never do such a thing. Yet she didn't know what she was basing that belief on, when she'd run again, last night. When in every way that mattered, she was still running.

So the only question was, what, exactly, had she been running from?

And where would it end? Where would she stop?

She didn't know. As ever, she wasn't sure she *wanted* to know.

But she did know she couldn't sit here, marinating in all of these revelations, without exploding. Or worse. She had to do something to escape her own head.

Kiara studied the collection of statues in the high-ceilinged, arched gallery that snaked along the outer lip of one of the lower levels of the palace. She'd wandered out of her rooms and through the palace, following whatever passage seemed most appealing, and had ended up here.

It was a striking, impressively unique room. The interior walls were rough and old, but the rest of the gallery was a modern confection of latticework and glass, showing the old clay statuary and assorted relics within to their best advantage. She leaned closer to a display of ancient-looking daggers, still deadly so many centuries since they'd been made.

And when she straightened, Azrin was beside her.

Her skin seemed to tighten over her bones, even as that familiar heat bloomed within her. Her body had no confusion where Azrin was concerned. Her body simply *wanted*.

"You have your very own museum here," she said before she knew she meant to speak, surprised to hear that light, sunny tone she would have said was lost to her trip from her lips so easily.

"It is part of the family collection," Azrin replied. When she glanced at him beside her, his gaze was narrow on hers. Considering. "Periodically we show pieces of it in the Royal Museum in Arjat an-Nahr." He reached down and ran a fingertip along the edge of an ancient scabbard. Kiara felt sensation swirl inside of her as if he'd touched her instead. "Though some pieces have been here for centuries."

He looked tired, she thought, her traitorous heart melting, even as her stomach twisted in a guilty little knot. His near-blue eyes seemed too dark, and his black hair looked rumpled, as if he'd been running his fingers through it. He wore another version of his all-black casual uniform, more warrior today than desert king—a pair of dark trousers and another torso-hugging T-shirt that made her hands itch to touch him. She smoothed down the front of the floor-length, casual sundress she wore instead, and found it a poor substitute.

"You certainly know how to hit on a girl." She tilted her head back and smiled slightly as she gazed at him. "Who can resist a man who claims an entire museum is only *part* of his family's private collection?"

His eyes met hers. Held. A moment passed, then another. Then, slowly, that almost-blue gaze began to gleam silver.

"It takes artifacts to win you, does it?" He spread out his hands, taking in the whole of the gallery. "Then I am your man." His mouth curved. "I can offer you the plunder of *several* museums."

"Tell me more," she said, aware of the way her heart beat a little bit harder, a little bit faster. She decided she might as well play the game the way they used to. Bold lies and brash claims. Whatever came to mind, purely to entertain. "I am nothing if not avaricious. I might as well be a magpie."

"My favorite quality in a woman," he said drily.

"I should think so," she agreed, and even laughed. "After all, you always know where you stand, don't you? When in doubt, throw some more priceless gems into the mix."

"Be still my heart."

She hadn't meant to move, hadn't realized they'd started walking together, until Azrin was gesturing for her to precede him out of the great glass doors that led out to a patio ringed with tall shade trees and a tall, gurgling fountain in the center. Kiara couldn't help but sigh in pleasure.

She walked to the fountain and sat on the wide lip of its basin, then trailed her fingers in the clear water. It was cool against her skin, but when she looked up at Azrin again, she knew the water was not why she had to restrain a shiver.

He stood with his hands thrust deep in his pockets, his uncompromisingly fierce face intense, his hard mouth merely hinting at the possibility of a curve. And his gaze seemed to move inside her like her own overheated blood. He was too beautiful, and somehow forbidding, too, and she couldn't quite bring herself to look away as she thought she should.

"I like that you're a king," she said in that flippant way that usually made him smile, and nearly did today. "It matches the palace. It's all very fairy tale-ish. And as a stereotypical magpie, I can't help but approve of all the implied royal shininess."

"Fairy tales tend to be inhabited by princes, not kings." There was that silver glint in his gaze, his mouth that little bit softer. "I think you have your happily ever afters confused."

"Are you saying I'm not Cinderella?" she asked in mock horror. She looked down at her sundress, the bright red fabric threaded through with hints of white flowers, all cascading to the feet she'd slipped into thonged sandals. "Does that make me Little Red Riding Hood instead?" She arched her brows when she looked back at him. "I think we both know what that makes you."

"You have no idea," he said, his voice like silk, as warm as the bright sun far above.

Time seemed to slip, to heat, to disappear into that sensual promise that hummed between them. Kiara had to look away to gain her balance. To remind herself why she should not—could not—sink into that promise and disappear.

"It must be better to be a king than a prince," she said instead, her voice huskier than it should have been. She found her teasing tone and matching smile hard to come by, but she managed both, somehow. "Everybody loves an upgrade."

Azrin looked at her for another long moment, this one threaded through with something far darker, a kind of smoke across the more familiar terrain of their wild chemistry.

"I'll share this with you," he said, as she'd begun to wonder if he planned to speak at all, "since you are a complete stranger to me. Just a girl I met in a museum, by chance, yes? It will be like confessing to the wind."

"You'll never see me again," she agreed, smiling. "As of tomorrow morning it will be like I never existed. You can tell me anything."

He rocked back on his heels, a curious sort of look on that powerful face, and a tension she didn't understand drawing the magnificent lines of his body tight. She felt her smile falter. He shrugged then, though he never looked away, and made a sound that was near enough to a laugh.

"I don't want to be king."

It was such a simple sentence. Such unremarkable words. He said it so quietly, almost casually, but Kiara knew better. She could feel the words like the bullets they were, one after the next. She felt every hair on her body seem to stand on end, and found it suddenly hard to swallow.

"But this is your destiny," she said, her voice little more than a whisper. "You have been preparing for it all of your life."

"It is my duty," he corrected her. His mouth curved then, but it was not a smile. "I have always done my duty, you understand. It defines me. Cambridge, Harvard Business School, the Khatan Investment Authority—all of these were carefully calculated steps toward the throne, decided upon by my father and his advisors, to make sure to craft me into a just and capable monarch, a credit to my family name in every respect." His hard mouth twisted. "My every move has been mapped out for me since the day I was born."

"Lucky for you that you excelled at all of those things," she said, trying to keep her tone light and not sure she succeeded.

"It wasn't luck," he said, not arrogant then so much as matter-of-fact, which made her heart seem to contract, then ache. "It was what was expected."

"Then I suppose we should be happy that you are so good at living up to expectations." She smiled again, though she suspected it was not a happy smile. "Some of us are not."

She searched his face, hardly recognizing the expression he wore, barely understanding the way he was looking at her.

"And then one day I met a girl in a café," he said quietly. Devastatingly. More bullets, and these hit hard, burrowed deep. "And she was completely unexpected."

"You should be careful about these girls you meet in all these public places." It was hard to sound teasing, mildly chastising, when there was such a great lump in her throat. When her chest hurt. "It can't possibly end well—and your reputation is sure to suffer."

"You are the only thing I ever wanted purely for myself," Azrin said, cutting through the game that easily, that sharply. Cutting it off. "The only thing that was not simply expected of me." His gaze was like fire, searing into her, until she felt all but cauterized. And breathless from the sting of it. He did not look away. He did not seem to move at all. "You are the only thing *I* chose."

She opened her mouth to speak, but no words came. And she felt that panic inside her, pushing through her limbs, making her shaky. Making her feel impossibly fragile. She wanted to move, to outrun it before it drowned her completely.

And she knew in a moment of perfect clarity that if he had not called her on it just the night before, she would have closed the distance between them and tried to soothe his words away with her mouth. Her hands. Any weapon at her disposal.

The revelation that he was absolutely right stunned her.

She had to blink it away like hot tears, burning at the backs of her eyes. Her heart was pounding too hard now, echoing in her ears and making her feel as if the whole earth, the stone palace and the pools beyond, rocked wildly beneath her. Even though she knew they did not. Even when she could hear the cheerful, oblivious splash of the fountain, like a merry little song that mocked what was happening inside her. She found herself on her feet, braced to run again, to bolt.

Only the fact he'd called her on that, too, stopped her.

And Azrin simply stood there, entirely too close, his arms crossed over his chest now, and watched her as if he could see this fight writ large across her face. She had no doubt that he could and that, too, made her wonder how she could possibly keep all the tears inside.

"You made me wish I could be a different man, Kiara," he said in that low voice that rolled through her, setting off more of those small earthquakes, leaving only debris and rubble behind. "I let myself imagine that we could simply be normal. Like anyone else. You made me forget, for five years, why that could never be. Left to my own devices, I would have played that game with you forever."

His gaze was hot, far hotter than the warm winter sun above them, and seemed to incinerate Kiara where she stood. She felt it—him—like a touch. As if he'd taken his elegant hands and run them all over her body. And as if he really had done exactly that, she felt her breasts grow heavy, the core of her grow damp. She felt that deep, low ache that only he could ease.

As if she could only process how much she wanted him, all the different layers of it, through the simplest, most direct method. As if sex could say everything she couldn't. As if it could bridge all of the spaces between them.

She felt frozen there before him, as surely as if he held her in his palms. Or pinned her to some wall somewhere.

He sighed slightly, as if he'd lost his own battle. As if he recognized hers. Then he reached over and curled his hands around her upper arms.

Don't, she thought desperately. *Please don't.*

But she didn't say the words out loud. Because she had no idea if they were directed to him— or to herself.

She could have moved away from him. She could have told him to stop. She knew she should have.

"Azrin…" she whispered.

But she didn't know whether she meant to beg him to stop, or to never stop, and the fact that she didn't know—that she couldn't tell—made her shake inside.

Again. Anew.

And that was when he bent and fixed his mouth to hers, hot and sweet and irresistible, and everything went wild and white.

He should not have tasted her. It was madness. He was a fool.

But he couldn't bring himself to stop.

He only knew that it took forever to claim her mouth with his. It had been so long. Too long. An eternity since he'd kissed her, held her. He exulted in the perfect fit of her against him, the sweetness of her curves beneath his hands, the promise in the tiny noises she whimpered into him as he slanted his mouth over hers and drank deep.

What could possibly matter, save this?

His body shouted the usual demands, as desperate for her as ever. But this time, he ignored the wild clamor of need. The driving beat of that passion that he could feel burning between them. The overpowering urge to drive deep inside of her and ride them both into blissful oblivion.

This time, he simply kissed her.

He sank his hands into the soft waves of her hair, anchoring her head into place, angling her face so he could find the perfect, slick fit of his mouth against hers. He let the kiss slow, go deep. She moved even closer, looping her arms around his neck and pressing her pert, plump breasts against his chest, making that demanding fire within him blaze ever higher, ever brighter.

He loved all of it. *Her.* He wanted to taste her from head to toe. He wanted to take that bright sundress off with his teeth. The ways he wanted her played on an endless, infinite loop inside of him, stoking that burning need, making him harder and wilder and that much more desperate for her.

And still he kissed her. As if there was nothing at all but this. But them.

As if there was no world at all, no demands. No

throne. No winery. No hotel room in Washington, shrouded in all that bitterness.

Only the shimmering, magical pools, the quiet song of the fountain behind them. Only the taste of her mouth. Only the perfection of the curve of her cheek beneath his palm.

Skin to skin. Her mouth under his. The sun and the sky and this. *Them.*

Her hands moved to stroke his jaw, his neck. He let one of his hands make that dangerous descent from the back of her head to the wickedly tempting line of her spine, tracing his way down until his fingers rested proprietarily at the small of her back.

My wife, he thought, a fierce and almost savage feeling pumping through him. *My queen.*

And he kissed her, over and over, endlessly, until he was drunk with it, intoxicated by her taste, by her closeness, by the small sounds she made, by the way he could not help but want her, love her, need her.

My Kiara.

He moved her away from him, settling her against the edge of the fountain again and moving to kneel before her. He ran his hands down her legs, all the way to her ankles, where he found his way beneath the hem of her dress. Then he retraced his path, skin against skin this time, and heard the ragged way she pulled in her next breath—so ragged it nearly qualified as a moan.

He'd take it.

He pulled the dress out of his way, baring her long, silky legs to his view. He followed the elegant line of one, using his lips and tongue, finding his way over the perfection of her calf to the sweet curve of her knee—and the delicate place behind it that made her shiver when he stroked it with his fingers. Then he moved higher, kissing his way up the delectable curve of her inner thigh. He found the scrap of silk and lace that stretched across her hips and pulled it down and then off, tossing it aside.

He looked up at her then. Her chest was heaving, her eyes wide. Her hands gripped the lip of the fountain so hard he could see a hint of white at her knuckles, and he could feel the way she trembled. He ran his palms up her legs again, shifting her slightly as he moved closer, then pulled up her legs to drape them over his shoulders, opening the very heart of her femininity to him.

She made a noise that could have been his name, her brown eyes black with passion. With the same need that clawed at him, dragging steel-tipped talons through his gut and demanding he take her, taste her, glut himself on her.

He leaned forward and licked his way into the molten core of her.

She shuddered and shook. She sobbed out his name, unmistakable this time. She moved against his mouth, riding his tongue, and he loved it, all of her. He anchored her hips with his hands and let her go wild against him, her back arching as her lovely body tensed. He worshipped her, lips and tongue and the faintest hint of his teeth, reveling in her incomparable taste. Her scent. Her hot, writhing pleasure.

She cried out his name once more—louder—and then she burst into flames all around him, nearly incinerating him, too, in the force of her sweet release.

It was not enough, Azrin thought then, as she slumped against him. It was never enough.

He moved to sit on the edge of the fountain

beside her, letting her lean heavily against his shoulder as she fought to come back to him.

It took two breaths. One, then another, and then her face paled.

She sat upright, pushing herself away from him. Her beautiful eyes darkened, and not with passion this time. She made a small, panicked sort of noise that seemed to hurt her, and thus him, and then she shoved herself away from him. She staggered slightly as she got to her feet, and the male in him found that leftover reaction far more satisfying than perhaps he should.

"Where are you going?" He could still taste her. It made him hard and edgy, neither of which he suspected would help him here. He wanted to pull her back against him and hold her, pull her down to the ground and take her until they were both limp and happy, but he imagined she wouldn't want that, either.

"Is this your plan?" she asked, her voice shaking. Her dark eyes looked haunted, despite the sunshine that poured down from above them. "You predicted this, didn't you? My token protest followed by sex... Isn't that what you said? How pleased you must be that I've fallen into line, just as you expected I would."

"Kiara."

There were spots of color high on her cheekbones now, and he saw the way she shivered, though it was nowhere near cold in the patio. She ignored him.

"Worst of all, you broke our agreement," she said in the same uneven voice. Her lips trembled. "And I let you."

"Was this not a gift?" he asked. "It was the very definition of a gift, I would have said."

"You know perfectly well that it was not." She bit at her lower lip. "The strings attached are practically visible."

"Kiara…" He said it again, as if her name would soothe her. Reach her. He had to order himself not to move, to simply sit and wait, and not use his body in a way she would claim was deliberate. As she claimed everything he did was deliberate. And so he only watched her, even as temper galloped through him, burning him alive. "I can't pretend I'm not in love with you."

He watched what looked too much like pure misery wash over her face, before she stepped back—as if she couldn't handle the words and needed to physically put space between her and their source. She shook her head slightly, as if she wanted to unhear them. As if she could. He saw her eyes grow bright and glassy, and knew she was fighting back tears. Her lips pressed together as if she was afraid of what she might say—or holding back sobs.

It killed him to see her like this.

"This shouldn't have happened," she rasped out.

"Is it really so terrible?"

He had the sense she was too fragile, now; too breakable, and he had to fight back everything inside of him that wanted to go to her, to protect her from whatever hurt her—even if it was herself. Or, worse, him.

"This is the problem," she managed to say after a moment, though her voice was choked. "No matter what I want, no matter what I think is right, I just…surrender to you. As if I have no will at all. I make a mockery of everything I believe to be true about myself every time I let you near me."

He ran his hands over his face, temper and

protectiveness in a pitched battle inside of him. She looked at him through bruised eyes, as if he truly was the big, bad wolf of all those European fables, and he found himself torn between the need to prove to her that he was not—and the more primal urge to simply show her his teeth.

"Kiara," he said, torn between a kind of exasperated amusement and something else, something deeper and, he thought, far sadder, "this is passion. This is love. This is what people all over the planet search for, fight for, kill for. How can you believe it's a problem?"

"It's easy for you to say that, isn't it?" She wrapped her arms around herself, as if she could ward off the shivers that way. Or him. "You always end up getting exactly what you want."

The things he wanted were so mundane, he thought, looking back at her from only a foot or two away, and yet, so far.

They were always so far away from each other.

He felt a profound sense of futility move through him then, and he shoved it aside. He refused to give up, to accept it. He wanted Kiara, in a hundred different ways. That was all. In his arms. In his bed. In his kingdom. But most of all—in his life. Why didn't she want the same things? Why was he the only one fighting for the two of them, for their marriage, while she seemed perfectly content to keep fighting him?

"You cannot honestly believe that any of this is *what I want*," he bit out, and there was no controlling the edge in his voice then. He didn't even try.

Her face seemed to crumple, and she took another step back. She shook her head again, as if trying to steady it, and she didn't meet his gaze.

He hated this. All of it. Himself most of all.

"I can't do this," she said in a low, thick voice. "I just can't."

He should let her go, he knew, though every part of him revolted at the very idea of it. She turned and started for the glass doors, hurrying as if she expected to be hauled back—or to collapse into tears. He knew he should say nothing at all. He should let her regroup, let her come up with a new suit of armor to wear around him. Let her build new walls. Produce new battalions to fight this endless war he was beginning to wonder if either of them would ever win.

He simply couldn't do it.

"Tell me," he said, his voice pitched to carry, laden with command, enough that she stopped in her tracks, one hand on the glass door in front of her. "When do you think we'll discuss the real issue here?"

She turned slowly. Carefully. It took her one breath, then another, to meet his gaze. Azrin stretched his legs out before him, crossing his ankles. He folded his arms over his chest. He watched her take that in, then gulp, and he accepted the possibility that he did not look as relaxed or inviting as he wished to appear.

"We've done nothing but discuss the real issues," she said after a moment, her head tilted slightly as if she was trying to read him. "Over and over again, in fact. We clearly do nothing save hurt each other. In the end, it's all a terribly painful waste of time."

"I couldn't agree more." Anticipation burned in him then, low and bright, and he felt everything in him still. Wait. Focus. She flinched slightly as if he'd surprised her.

"Right." She looked confused for a moment, then inexpressibly sad, but she pulled it all in and managed to produce that neutral, unassuming expression instead. The one she'd worn all over the world, charming everyone in her wake. The one he knew was nothing but a mask. "I'm glad."

"Let's put an end to it, shall we?" He could hear the darkness in his own voice, the kick of his temper beneath it. He had no doubt she could, too. "Why bother to keep fighting? As you say, it does nothing at all but make everything worse. We had a lovely five years, didn't we?"

He almost stopped then, as a terrible look flashed through her beautiful eyes. Something far worse than simple pain or temper. It almost undid him. But she wiped it away. She squared her shoulders and tilted up her chin, as if she expected he might swing at her next. As if he already had.

"We did," she said, that telling huskiness in her voice.

"Then all I require of you is one simple thing," he said. As if it would be easy. "The answer to a single question. No more and no less, and then we can be done with this. Once and for all."

"Ask it." Her voice bordered on harsh, but he could hear the emotion that simmered beneath it. He could see it in the places her mask failed, somehow, to cover. He smiled.

And then he lifted one hand and beckoned her close with a regal flick of his fingers. "Come here," he said.

He didn't pretend it was anything less than a command. And she didn't pretend she wasn't aware of it. He could see the trembling she fought to keep under control. He could see the shifting tides of feeling in her dark brown gaze. He watched the war she fought with herself—to take that next breath, to walk toward him with something less than her usual grace, to keep moving toward him when he knew very well it was the last thing she wanted to do.

"Closer," he said when she stopped a few feet away. He could read the mutinous expression on her face then, easily. "You look as if you expect me to bite you."

"I'm not ruling it out." But she set her jaw visibly and took the necessary steps toward him, putting herself within arm's reach.

She stood there, her hands at her sides even as every single part of her vibrated with tension. And that underlying panic. He could see it as clearly as if she'd hung signs announcing it around her neck. He was tempted to let her stew in it. He almost did.

"There," he said finally. With entirely too much satisfaction. "Was that so hard?"

"As a matter of fact, it was." She shifted from one foot to the other. "Is that your question?"

"Not exactly." He wanted to touch her. He forced himself to restrain the urge. "Though it will lead us into it nicely."

"I don't want to play this game, whatever it is." Her voice was hoarse again. It made him wonder what showed on his face. What she saw of that darkness he was holding tight within him. That fury.

"One question," he said softly. Almost kindly. "That's all. You need only answer it honestly and I'll set you free, if that is what you want."

Again, that misery that she fought so hard to hide moved over her face, but she nodded anyway. As if she had to fight herself to do even that.

"It's very simple." He leaned in close and made sure every word counted. Made sure she was watching him. Hearing him. Made sure there could be no mistake about this. "Just tell me what it is you're running from."

CHAPTER NINE

IT WAS if he'd sucked all the air out of the world.

Kiara stared at him, stricken. And then her heart pounded into her stomach like a sledge-hammer, and she wondered if she was going to be sick. One beat, then another, and she still wasn't sure. She felt a wild, terrible heat engulf her. It was as if he'd pried her open and exposed the deepest, darkest parts of her to a blistering light, and she hated it. She hated it, she hated him, *she couldn't breathe—*

She swayed on her feet, battling what seemed like stars behind her eyes. She wanted to back away from him, but knew that would only prove his point. It was harder to stand there, harder to *keep* standing there, than it should have been. Than it was to do anything else, including keep-ing herself upright and in one piece, somehow, despite the stunning blow he'd dealt her.

She still couldn't seem to catch her breath.

How does he know? some voice inside her asked in a panic, but the part of her that wasn't surprised—the part of her that had, perhaps, been expecting something like this on some level— simply *hurt*.

"I'm not running," she managed to say in someone else's voice, though she knew those were her lips that moved. That forced out automatic denials even she did not believe. "I'm right here."

But Azrin only watched her, his storm-tossed eyes entirely too knowing, and she let out a small noise that was much too close to a sob.

She felt dizzy again. *Still.* Her mind flooded with a burst of images, memories, cascading through her, one on top of the next. All those things she didn't want to think about. All those difficult truths she didn't want to face. Everything that had brought her here. It all seemed to whirl inside her like some kind of vicious tornado, spinning around, coiling tighter, ever more dangerous and out of control—until she thought she might burst.

Until she thought she *wanted* to burst, because that might stop the awful spinning.

"You're the one who changed, Azrin," she

whispered, desperate to say or do *something* that might ease the pressure inside her. Terrified that if she didn't push it away somehow, it would eat her alive. Far too worried that it already had. "I didn't change at all. Things were perfect the way they were."

She hardly knew what she was saying, but she couldn't seem to stop herself. Azrin shifted then, lifting a hand to stroke his hard jaw, his eyes glittering as they narrowed in on her.

"I thought so, as well," he said, and she didn't know why she thought he was so calm when she could hear that harsh undercurrent in his voice, when she could see the darkness in that near-blue gaze. When she could feel it sear into her skin, like some kind of brand. "But was it really?"

"Do we have to tear apart our history, too?" she demanded, that great emptiness yawning open inside of her again, this time with teeth. "Are you determined to see to it that we have nothing to salvage from this at all?"

She raised her hands to smooth down her dress, as if that would save her, and was surprised to feel that they trembled. And she remembered with perfect, unpleasant clarity that sense of relief she'd often felt when she'd left Azrin in some or other city to return to her career, that feeling she'd tried so hard to stuff down deep inside her and pretend wasn't happening.

Because he was so demanding. So...*much*. Because she lost her head over him so easily, so totally.

The guilt swamped her now as if it was new. And she couldn't pretend that she didn't know what it was, that primal urge to return to the life she knew and could control, the life she already knew all the twists and turns of, having watched her mother live it once already. She remembered how decadent it had always felt to spend more than a few days with him at any one time, how far she'd felt herself fall into him whenever he was near—and yet how she'd never forgot that it was always only temporary. She'd wanted it to stay that way. She'd made sure to keep it that way, hadn't she?

She'd never wanted to disappear so far into him that she'd be unable to find her way back. She'd never let herself come close.

"What are you so afraid of?" he asked now. She could hear the torment in that low, commanding tone. She felt a matching agony twist inside her, stealing what little breath she could manage.

And suddenly it was as if she could speak now, or die of it.

As if there was no other choice.

"You." It was barely a whisper, barely audible, but she knew he heard her. When he only watched her, his eyes hooded and painfully dark, one of her hands crept up to press hard against her chest as if she could soothe the frantic beating of her heart. "Me, when I'm with you." She searched his face, so fierce and proud. "But I think you already know that."

She backed up then, no longer caring what it proved about her. One step, then another, and still Azrin did nothing but watch her do it. *Let* her do it. And the scant bit of breathing room didn't help at all. She might as well have been caged between his palms. Threaded around his elegant fingers.

Some part of her was, she knew. And always would be, no matter what happened here.

Why did acknowledging that inevitability make her want to weep?

"I have been proving myself to you since the day we met," he said, a certain hardness in his voice now, betraying that cold temper of his she could sense if not see. "But it doesn't matter, does it? You decided long ago that I would leave you, and you have been punishing me for it ever since."

"That's not true!" She flung the words at him, her knees weak beneath her, her stomach lurching. "We have wholly incompatible lives!"

Azrin shook his head. A single, definitive jerk. Dismissing her protests that easily.

"If I could give up this kingdom for you, I would," he said, his gaze connecting with hers and making her shiver. "I would grow grapes in your precious valley. I would learn the land. And it would be a good life, Kiara. Don't think for a moment I haven't thought about it."

"You have not," she hissed at him, shaking off the images his words conjured in her head, refusing to let herself dwell on them—or on the part of her that balked at the idea of this proud, regal man in any role but the one he had. He was a king, not a winemaker. The idea that he would consider the alternative made her angry, suddenly. "You want me to believe you have fantasies of turning into Harry Thompson? Of course you don't. Don't patronize me."

"I'm not that man," he bit out, the price of his iron control visible in every hard line of his body, his tight jaw, the arms that seemed to clench where he still held them crossed over his chest. All of that temper he managed to hold in reserve, she thought, when she felt utterly undone. "I can't be. I can't abandon this country, no matter how much I love you. But there's one thing I can't manage to understand, Kiara, no matter how many times I work this all through in my head."

He paused, as if to make sure she was listening to him. She had to grit her teeth against the roar of the tornado inside her, the way it clawed to get out, the things she was afraid she might say. His head tilted slightly to one side, studying her.

"Why don't you love me enough to consider the same sacrifice?" he asked.

It felt as if an electric current pulsed through her, making everything burn bright and then scream with the same deep ache. And she was no longer at all sure that she was going to survive this.

"I love you enough to think we should do better than tear each other apart!" she threw at him, that wild storm bursting out of her, no longer something she could even pretend to control. "I love you enough to know I can't be what you want—and that you want far more than I'm able to give. I love you enough—"

"Kiara."

Her name was a brisk, implacable command this time, and she despaired of herself when she heeded it and fell silent. He was so still, all that seething ruthlessness firmly held in check, right there, right in front of her, behind his dangerous gaze. All that intense male power focused on her, until she felt crowded out of her own body. Panic beat in her, through her. That harsh electricity burned.

"Hear me," he ordered her, very distinctly. Every inch of him the king. Nothing soft. All fierce lines and ruthless certainty. "I am not your father."

And it was too much.

Finally.

It was as if those words detonated a bomb deep inside her, and everything simply *exploded*. It was all the worse because it was so silent, and so total. Her toes to her hip bones to her elbows to her head—all blown away. All lost.

The buzzing in her ears shifted, liquid and sickening, to intense dizziness. Her knees gave out from beneath her. And for the first time in her life, Kiara stopped fighting and simply…fell.

But Azrin caught her.

She never saw him move. She simply found herself in his arms, cradled against the immovable wall of his chest. She realized she was crying, then; great, body-racking sobs that she thought might wreck her completely—might tear her into a thousand pieces were he only to loosen his hold.

But he didn't.

He stooped and swept her into his arms, and then carried her over to the bench that stood in a corner of the patio, shaded from the sun above with a straight view out over the sparkling pools below.

And he sat there, holding her, for what seemed to Kiara like a very long time.

She simply cried.

She let it all out, things she hadn't known she was holding on to and the things she'd planned to keep her fingers tightly clenched around forever. She sobbed against his chest, her hands over her face as if she could hide, now, when he'd already seen everything. The very worst of her. She simply wept, while he whispered soothing Arabic words she didn't understand and kissed her gently, softly on her temple. Her cheek. The backs of the hands she tried to use as some kind of shield.

She cried until she felt empty of it all, hollowed out, but this time not in that terrible, aching way. As if she had finally cleared the space. As if she was made new somehow. And when she opened her eyes again and pulled in a deep breath, there was Azrin.

Waiting for her, as he always did. The truth of that seemed to move over her, through her, like light.

"They planned out their whole life," she said, her voice thick with the aftereffects of so many tears. So much poison. She wiped at her face, curling toward him even more, as if she could never be close enough. "They were going to work in the vineyards together, raise a family. Live off the land and turn it into something bigger than them. My father was the one with all the dreams."

She shook her head. "And they ended up with so little time together. Not even three years."

He smoothed a hand over her hair, and pressed a new kiss to her forehead.

"I expect you to disappear," she whispered. "All it takes is one car accident, and everything is changed. Forever."

"I know." He held her closer, tighter. "I know."

And there was a peace, somehow, in the promises he didn't make, the future he didn't pretend to know. The tacit admission that no one could know. It seemed to soothe something raw that had lived inside her for far too long.

His strong, magnificent body surrounded her, and Kiara couldn't help but revel in it. She might have been conflicted all this time, but her body was not. As ever, it molded to him, took his strength and heat and wrapped it around her, making her feel safe. Protected. *Loved.*

She understood, then, what she hadn't before. What all their heat, their white-hot chemistry and deep sensual connection, had disguised. Or helped confuse. That she had always felt safe with this man, from the moment she'd met him, or she would never have let him buy her that long-ago coffee.

And it was that very feeling that had always terrified her so profoundly. Because if she lost the man who made her feel like this, as if she was finally home whenever and wherever they were so long as he was near, then what? How could she recover from that kind of body blow? Look at what had happened to her mother. How shut down and closed off she'd become, even from her own daughter.

So she had prepared for his loss in advance. She had kept herself at arm's length, emotionally and physically, which had been easy to do with their demanding schedules over the years. They'd been on a perpetual honeymoon. But come the real marriage, the day-to-day living together, the reality of duties and responsibilities with no escape? It had all become that much more dangerous for her. That much more terrifying.

She'd had to face the fact that if she let herself go—if she relinquished her escape hatch—she would be entirely at the mercy of this man. Utterly submerged in him, as she'd always fought so hard to prevent.

And if he left when she'd given up everything else? When she'd finally let herself become dependent on him emotionally—finally allowed herself to trust him? How could she possibly survive it? She'd never wanted to find out.

The insight shook her down her toes.

"Azrin..."

She said his name as if she was tasting it for the first time, and his hard mouth curved. His near-blue eyes saw too deep, too far, but this time, she didn't fear what he might find. This was the beginning of their marriage, she thought. Five years later than it should be, a bit hard-won and battle scarred, but it was theirs.

And she would fight for it with everything she had. Everything she was.

Even if she didn't know how.

"I don't even know what to promise you," she whispered now, holding his beloved face in her hands. "I don't even know where to start."

"Try to do this with me without running away from me every time you get scared." His voice was rough, his gaze intense. He brushed her hair from her face, then pressed a slow, sweet, intoxicating kiss to her mouth. It was like a vow. "All you have to do is try, Kiara. That's where we start."

* * *

And so she tried. They tried together.

One day bled into the next, golden sun and crisp blue sky. They ate grand Khatanian feasts in the shade and swam in the pools. They sat out on the balconies and wrapped themselves around each other every night as they slept together in the grand old bedroom reserved for the king.

They talked. Of everything and nothing. They played their old, familiar games and they carefully, cautiously, built new bridges between them in the fragile peace they'd found. And they *wanted*. She knew exactly how much he wanted her, because she wanted him in the same way. It was sex and need and that tautly wound, inexhaustible passion that burned between them and was never fully sated. Never burned out.

And they loved each other with it, again and again. They explored each other's bodies as if they were brand-new to each other. Azrin took her with his usual command and inventive flair wherever they found themselves. She had her way with him in the dark, intimate embrace of the hot pools deep in the mountainside, quiet and fierce, surrounded by a hundred candles. He returned the favor in the bright white heat of midday, her hands braced against the balustrade while Azrin moved, so hot and so devastatingly sensual, behind her.

And all the while, the pools sighed and murmured all around them. Birds sang strange and lovely choruses from the trees and the winter sun beamed down bright and warm, surrounding them in a bright cocoon of sunshine and song. It was magical. Some kind of sorcery, and he was in the center of it.

Kiara felt as if she'd been transported to a different world. A fantasy world, where a place like this could exist at all and a man like this could look at her with that silver gleam in his eyes that she knew was a smile, and she could let herself feel nothing at all but treasured. She had to keep reminding herself that this was no fantasy—this was real. This was their life.

This is where it starts, she told herself every day, like a prayer. *This is our marriage.*

And slowly, carefully, she started to let herself believe that it might work. That she could trust him, and love him, and that there was no need to hold some part of her in reserve. That she could trust in what they had enough to do without her escape route.

Every day they spent together, she believed it a little bit more.

Then, one day, as they sat together on the great slab of smooth rock that served as the palace's beach, beneath the rustling palm trees, there was a noise from high above them. At first it didn't make sense, to hear such a strange, mechanical sound in the midst of so much natural splendor. Kiara had the mad notion that it was her heart, so loud this time that even he heard it and frowned. But then she recognized the sound she was hearing and looked up.

A helicopter. Sleek and black and clearly military.

And it was coming down for a landing.

By the time it did, Azrin had turned to stone. It didn't matter that he wore nothing but a swimming costume. He might as well have been draped in finery and sitting amidst the gold and precious stones in his throne room, complete with his crown and a selection of royal advisors.

He was once and again the king, Kiara thought. The reality of their lives had intruded once more.

As it always will, she reminded herself. She watched the way he stood there, so coldly regal and detached, waiting to hear whatever terrible news they had come in so dramatic fashion to deliver to him here in this secret corner of his kingdom.

And this time, when she told herself she could do it, she believed she really could. *She would.* Because what mattered was not what life threw at them, but that they lived it together.

Surely if she'd learned anything, it was that.

"Your Majesties," the soldier intoned respectfully, sinking to his knees in front of them when he climbed out of the helicopter, but when he lifted his gaze from the ground he looked only at Azrin. Who nodded as only a king could, no more than a supremely arrogant tilt of his head.

"A thousand apologies for disturbing you, Sire, but you are wanted in Arjat an-Nahr." The soldier cleared his throat, his agitation plain, making Kiara clench her hands into fists against the tension—but Azrin only waited, as if he already knew whatever news the man brought. As if nothing could shock him. "It is your father."

* * *

The old king had slipped into a coma, far sicker, it turned out, than he had been prepared to admit when he'd relinquished the throne.

"It is difficult to say," the doctor told Azrin as they stood next to the old man's bed. Azrin could hardly look at the frail figure before him; in his head, his father was still so large, so colorful. Belligerent and bombastic. Occasionally cruel. Not this tiny man, finally succumbing to an illness he'd already beat back once before, reduced to tubes and machines and hovering medical personnel. "It's possible he could pull out of this, but it would only be a reprieve. Your father, Your Majesty, is gravely ill."

"How ill?" he asked, his tone short. The doctor did not seem to notice—or think it unusual if he did.

"I would be shocked if he wakes up from this coma," the doctor said after a brief pause. The man shifted position, as if he fully expected to be struck down for what he was about to say, but squared his shoulders and went ahead anyway, and Azrin found he liked him for it. "And it would be nothing short of miraculous if he lives out the week."

Azrin stared down at his father for a long time. "I understand," he said.

And he did. He understood his role, his place, his duty, in a way he hadn't before. It was as if a fog had suddenly lifted to reveal the bright glare of the desert sun, and he could see clearly for the first time in years. He could see exactly what he was doing, and what he needed to do.

He could see far too much.

It had been a shock for him to take the throne so soon, when he hadn't thought he'd have to face that responsibility for years. Decades, even. Perhaps he'd even panicked, loath as he was to admit that even to himself. He had lost himself in those five years with Kiara, and he couldn't regret it even now. He'd loved that fantasy version of himself—a man who could travel the world on some kind of an extended honeymoon, only intermittently accountable to his people. Before her, there had been only his duty and his future. But with her, he'd wanted nothing at all save that beautiful present to continue indefinitely.

He had let himself forget.

And then, when it was time, he had taken the crown knowing full well his father was still here. Sick, but capable of offering his opinions, the canny insights that had helped make him so formidable over the course of his reign. Even if Azrin disagreed with him or thought him depressingly hidebound, as he often did, the old man was there. It wasn't all Azrin's responsibility. For all intents and purposes, he'd had a king in reserve.

It had allowed him to make promises about reforms while concentrating instead on his own marriage above all things. On some level, he had still been lost. Still behaving like the prince he'd been.

But now there was only Azrin. It was life without a safety net, a reign all his own, whether he was ready for it or not.

He stood back as his father's wives came into the room. He caught his mother's gaze, not surprised to see she'd broken with her customary impassivity and was sobbing like the others. She came to him, burying her face against his shoulder. He almost wished he could allow himself that kind of release, but then, he was no longer a son, a brother, a husband.

He was the king. First, last, always. It was time he came to terms with that.

"I am lost!" his mother wailed against his shoulder. "We are all lost!"

Azrin murmured something soothing, his eyes on his father's other two wives. They, too, looked as destroyed as his own mother sounded. It was more than grief, he thought; it was a sharp, encompassing panic, and an anguish, as if they were lying in that bed along with Zayed. Or as if they wanted to be.

"We will get through this," he told his mother, as more of that unwelcome clarity hit him.

"There is no *through*," she said dully, her face twisting into something unrecognizable. And Azrin realized he had never seen his mother without his father. That she was unintelligible to him without the force of his father behind her. "What am I without him?"

He could not answer her.

Out in the private waiting room the hospital had set aside for the royal family, all of his sisters gathered with their husbands and children, all of them focused on each other and their shared worry, their grief. Some of his sisters wept. His brothers-in-law, most of them high-ranking members of his government, spoke in low voices to each other. They were indistinguishable from one another in their particular high-class Khatanian way. He could close his eyes and pick out their roles, each person's status, their place in the family, simply by the way they spoke.

And in the corner, sitting on her own, her hands clenched tightly before her, standing out from the crowd like a beacon of light, *his* light, was Kiara.

She would never fit in here, not completely, and there was no pretending that was not precisely why he'd been so drawn to her. She would never blend. She'd been a vibrant splash of color against the wet and gray of the Melbourne laneway all those years ago. Against the demands of his life. She still was.

She was nothing like his sisters, his mother, his father's other wives. She was not from this world, *his world*, and she never would be. She had been right to accuse him of trying to force her into a role that didn't fit her at all. She'd been right about a lot of things.

I don't want to be your mother, she'd told him.

And if he was honest, if he listened to her rather

than his own selfish need for her, he didn't want her to be his mother, either. He didn't want her to face the prospect of his own death with so little strength at her disposal. He didn't want her to face anything like that. He wanted her strength, her fire. He couldn't imagine her without it.

If you love me, she had told him in Washington, *let me go*.

He had still been holding on to so many things then, and she was one of them. She was the emblem of the life he might have lived if he was someone else. And he'd had the opportunity to live it for five glorious, perfect years. But there were far greater concerns than his heart. It should never have been a factor in the first place.

It was long past time he grew up.

As if Kiara could feel him, her gaze rose and met his from across the room, and he felt it like a touch. Like her hands across his skin, teasing and tormenting him, bringing him ever closer to that sweet madness. Like those perfect, endless days at the pools that he understood, too late now, were their last.

Because he knew what he had to do. What he

should have done from the start, had he not been so weak. So inexcusably, damagingly selfish.

"Your Majesty," an attendant said respectfully as Kiara arrived back at the palace after another long day at hospital. "Your mother waits for you in your chamber."

Kiara had smiled automatically as the woman started to speak, but it took long moments for the words to penetrate. Even when they did, they made no sense.

"My mother?" Kiara asked, baffled. "Here?"

The attendant only nodded, and Kiara walked the rest of the way to her rooms rather more quickly than she might have otherwise, mystified.

Sure enough, Diana stood out on the private terrace that linked Kiara's suite to Azrin's, gazing out over the sea. Kiara blinked, unable to make sense of her mother's presence in a place thousands of miles and halfway across the globe from where it ought to be. She repressed the urge to rub at her eyes.

Diana turned as Kiara walked out through the glass doors and smiled in her enigmatic way, looking as elegant and unreachable in a flowing caftan as she did in her denim jeans or occasional ball gowns back in Australia. The stars seemed particularly bright above them, as if in counterpoint to the jutting skyscrapers that trumpeted Khatan's wealth and financial prowess from the city center far below the palace.

"It really is lovely here," Diana said with a smile that seemed almost bittersweet.

Kiara closed the distance between them, frowning. She could think of too many horrible reasons for her mother to appear in person here, rather than simply sending one of her usual emails or even making a phone call. Too many to count.

"What are you doing here?" she asked, tripping over her words as her imagination ran away with all the possibilities. "Has something happened?"

It was Diana who frowned then, her elegant brow wrinkling in apparent confusion. She shifted back as Kiara approached, and tilted her head slightly to one side, as if Kiara was behaving oddly and required observation.

"Azrin had me come," she said. Her tone indicated this should have been common knowledge. "I didn't think it was meant to be a surprise, was it?"

"Because of his father?" Kiara couldn't remember her mother and King Zayed ever speaking, aside from a few formalities at the wedding. Why would she come to see him at hospital? More to the point, why would Azrin ask her to come?

"No, Kiara." Diana's frown deepened. "Because of you."

Her gaze turned something very like *kind* then, and far too knowing, and Kiara felt a cold chill wash over her, into her, down deep into her bones.

No.

She could think of only one good reason that her mother would look at her like that. Only one. But it was impossible. Not after everything they'd been through. Not now, when she'd finally stopped wanting exactly this.

"I'm fine," she said, as if to stave it off, this thing that was happening here, but there was a deafening sort of buzzing sound, and it took her longer than it should have to realize it was only in her head.

Diana smiled then, with compassion—but no surprise. No surprise at all.

But it was impossible.

Kiara didn't realize she'd spoken out loud, until her mother's smile deepened.

"No, darling," Diana said gently. "Don't you see? He's finally set you free."

CHAPTER TEN

No.

The word cracked in her like a thunderclap. Kiara stared at her mother for a single, stunned moment, then abruptly she turned on her heel and started for the doors to her room. Fury and purpose coursed through her blood, heating her from the inside out.

"I'm sorry you came all this way," she said over her shoulder, but there was no helping it. Not when everything inside her was focused on what Azrin must have said—what he must have been thinking—to get Diana to come here. And here she had been trying to give him distance to deal with his father's condition! "I'm afraid it was a wasted trip."

She was almost to the door that led back out into the main part of the palace when her mother caught up with her.

"Kiara!"

The way Diana said her name suggested she'd said it more than once. Kiara stiffened, but she turned back around anyway—though it went against everything inside her to do it when adrenaline was pumping through her, making her feel jittery. Making her want to run through the palace and find him. Fight him.

No, she thought again, furiously. *He is not doing this. He is* not *doing this.*

"Perhaps you should take a moment," Diana suggested, in that carefully neutral tone of hers that indicated she expected Kiara to erupt into temper. Or that she thought Kiara already had. "And really think things through."

"What do you think I need to think through?" Kiara asked, fighting to keep all that adrenaline out of her voice, all of her mounting tension to herself. She saw her mother's expression and accepted that she'd failed.

Diana pulled in an audible breath, and a wave of sadness—or perhaps it was regret—washed over Kiara as it occurred to her that her mother was nervous. That they were both so eternally nervous around each other.

"It seems to me that your relationship with

Azrin has been, since the start, based very much on spontaneous, emotional decisions," Diana said, her voice neutral as ever—only that quick breath before to betray her. She held up a hand as if staving off an argument. "That is not a judgment. Merely an observation." She took another breath. "Perhaps you have an opportunity here to pause and reflect. To think about what you really want."

Kiara remembered, then, the way she'd left things with her mother. The terrible thing she'd said to her—even if, a small voice whispered, it might have been true. And yet despite that, Azrin had called her and she had come. Kiara supposed that said more about her mother than she had ever been willing to admit to herself. That Diana loved her in her own way. That she always had.

It made her profoundly sad that it was such a novel thought. And there was no reason at all that she shouldn't face this relationship with honesty, too. No reason she shouldn't try to see if she could make it that little bit better between them. If it was possible.

"You and I are so much alike, aren't we?" she asked softly. Diana's eyebrows shot high, and her

careful expression melted away into something…
honest, at least. If wary. Kiara lifted a shoulder.
"Neither one of us was asked if we'd like to take
over Frederick Winery. You felt you had to live
up to the Frederick legacy. So do I—except I feel
I have to live up to all of that and your expectations. The sacrifices you made for me."

"My sacrifices were my choice," Diana said
stiffly. "But it was never my intention to force
you into a role you hated. I could have sworn you
enjoyed what you did, Kiara. I know you did."

"I did," Kiara agreed evenly. "I like the business world. I like working. I particularly like the
wine business." Diana had begun to nod, as if
Kiara was making her argument for her. Kiara
shook her head. "But I am the Queen of Khatan."

It was the first time she'd said it like that. As
if she was claiming it. She felt a deep kick of
something like power, as if she was connecting,
finally, with what this new life, this marriage,
would entail. As if she was finally accepting that
this was hers.

He was not doing this to her. Not now.

"Kiara…" Diana began, frowning the way she
did when she was searching for another line of

argument. Another approach, another rational-
ization.

"Why do we both have such a narrow view of
things?" Kiara asked then. "Why do we both assume that because something has always been
done one way, it can only be done that way?
That's not how we make our best wines, is it?"

Diana only gazed back at her, no doubt trying to figure out where she was going, what
she meant. Kiara wasn't sure she knew, but she
pressed on.

"I can't be the vice president of Frederick
Winery and also the queen of Khatan," Kiara
said, and she knew it was true. Some part of her
mourned that deeply. Some part of her wanted to
cling to that old life out of fear, just as she always
had. But the rest of her wanted whatever came
next—as long as it came with Azrin. "But that's
not to say I can't sit on the board of directors. I
just can't be as involved in the day-to-day running of the winery as I used to be. It's not all or
nothing, is it? As if without me as vice president,
Frederick Winery will fall off the face of the
planet?" She laughed quietly. "It's been running

just fine without me these last months, hasn't it? Too well, one might say."

Diana let out a small breath that could have been a sigh. She was still impossible to read. Kiara reminded herself that she would always be Diana, no matter what understanding they might reach.

"Do you think this will make you happy?" Diana asked after a moment, shaking her head as if Kiara had disappointed her yet again. But, Kiara thought, if she had—that was all on Diana. There was nothing she could do about it. And she could no longer tear herself apart in the trying. "Disappearing into this world of his?"

"Did it make you happy when you did it?" Kiara countered, and then felt a sharp pang of instant regret when her mother blanched. "I'm not trying to be cruel," she continued, though she felt uneven, off balance and wasn't entirely sure what she was trying to do. "I promise you, I don't want to disappear. And you don't have to, either, you know. If you don't want to anymore. You can choose something else."

And so can I, she thought, and it was as if she

was finally giving herself permission. Or forgiveness.

It was Diana's turn to blink. To stare at Kiara for a long moment, as if she didn't know who Kiara was—or had no idea what she was talking about.

"You had dreams," Kiara reminded her, her voice urgent with emotions she couldn't name—she could only feel the long overdue truth of them. "You can still make them come true."

"Because you think the fairies will come and run the winery, do you?" Diana asked, but Kiara heard the thickness in her voice that she was trying to conceal beneath that touch of asperity.

"Go find a bed-and-breakfast on a lonely spit of land somewhere and see what happens," Kiara suggested in a voice gone hoarse. "The winery will be fine. We'll make sure it's fine."

She felt the surge of heat at the back of her eyes, and could see an answering brightness in her mother's, and for the first time in her life, wished that they were the sort of women who embraced.

But maybe this was where it all started, the relationship they should have had all these years. This moment, right here.

"You don't have to prove anything in those vineyards any longer, Mum," she whispered, using the familiar name she hadn't said out loud since she was a child. And there might have been tears that they were both too stubborn to let fall, but they were both smiling, too. "And neither do I."

She found him in his private study, hidden away in the diplomatic wing of the palace, where she had never known him to go except in the daytime. She stood in the doorway for a moment, taking a breath or two to simply drink him in.

He looked far too tired, if still so beautiful, his fierce face looking more weary than ferocious tonight, his hard mouth a firm, grim sort of line. He was sprawled back in the oversized armchair that sat at an angle before a fireplace. He was wearing one of his exquisite dark suits and he hadn't even bothered to loosen his tie.

He was staring straight ahead, as if he saw ghosts standing before him in the empty room. As if he was the loneliest man alive.

"You should be gone by now," he said without

looking up. Kiara's heart gave a great thump in her chest.

"I'm not being sent off in the night," she replied tartly. "Under cover of darkness, as if I should be ashamed."

"Tomorrow morning, then." Still, he did not look at her. Though she saw the way his mouth tightened, and she could sense the way his temper coiled in him, raw and close to the surface.

"What happened to the two of us doing this together?" she demanded. "With no one running away?" She thought he meant to speak, but then he seemed to think better of it. She moved farther into the room. "Instead you called my mother?" she asked, her tone one of utter disbelief.

He made a noise then that was somewhere between a snort and a laugh.

"I imagined her triumph at the end of our marriage would make the long flight seem to race by," he said in a voice too dark to truly be dry.

Kiara kept moving until she stood before him, looking down at that marvelous body of his, long and lean and sleek. What was wrong with her, she wondered, that he could order her away with every appearance of sincerity and she could still want him so badly?

He took his time raising his gaze to hers. She felt the heat of it, the way he dragged his eyes along every curve of her body. The tailored dress she'd worn to the hospital suddenly felt unduly confining. The modest neck and fashionably cinched waist seemed impossibly constricting, as if it was shrinking against her skin as she stood there.

But she knew better. She knew it was Azrin.

He finally met her gaze, his own dark, stormy. His harsh mouth betrayed no curve, not even the faintest hint of one. He looked edgy and danger-ous tonight, too much a warrior, too unpredict-able a man.

"Do you need to hear me say it?" he asked, in a tone she hardly knew, harsh and almost cold. "I release you." His voice was distinct. Precise. "Go. Be whatever you want, wherever you want. This time I will not follow you. This time I will let you be. You have my word."

She would have been heartsick to hear him say such things, she recognized from some distant place, had she had any intention at all of obeying him. As it was, she only stood there, staring down at him—challenging him.

"You're giving up?" she asked. Her brows arched up. "After all your talk at the pools. Is this is your revenge?"

"The pools are not reality." His voice was frigid, but his eyes were hot. He sat forward as if to emphasize the point. "And neither are we."

"But I thought—"

"What is this?" He sounded impatient, but the way he looked at her said something else, and she clung to that. He rose from the chair then, so they were standing too close together, and frowned down at her. "I thought you would rejoice in your freedom. I thought this would give you the excuse you needed to leave here and never look back."

"You thought wrong," she retorted. She wanted to touch him, but held herself in check. "Not the first time."

"I've finally realized that none of this matters, Kiara," he growled down at her. "You, me—this was nothing more than a fantasy." His jaw was like granite. "I've always known exactly what my life must be, what it will entail and what I will have to do to serve this country as my family has done for generations."

His mouth twisted then, and it was still no smile. It made Kiara's stomach turn over. He reached over and took her upper arms in his hands, but not, she understood, in a particularly tender manner. She still bloomed beneath his touch.

"I am a selfish man," he said bitterly. "I always have been where you are concerned. And you were right. I knew what kind of woman I should have married. One who would have understood what was expected. One who would have welcomed the weight of it all. But I had to have you instead."

He leaned closer, and his eyes were the blackest she'd ever seen them. They made her shiver.

"And look what I've done to you," he whispered, his voice like a lash.

He let go of her then and she fell back a step, feeling dizzy. She was not prepared for this. For what it meant if he gave up. If he stopped fighting for this, for them. For her. But she remembered everything that had happened at the pools, everything they'd discovered, and she knew that if she had to be the one to fight, she would. For him. For them.

For as long as it took.

"I don't want you to let me go." She searched his face as he stared at her. She watched the way he raked his fingers through his thick black hair. The way he shook his head. The way he yanked his tie from around his neck as if he, too, felt constricted.

Perversely, that gave her hope.

"I may not have choices," he said in a low voice, "but you do. If you stay here, I can't promise that these roles won't eat us alive. I expect they will. They already have. And then what?"

"I don't want to disappear." She moved toward him, deliberately, forcing his gaze to hers. "But I'm not afraid of that any longer, not the way I was. You asked me to trust you, Azrin, and I do."

"You say that," he said quietly, his voice laced with regret, and that underlying bitterness, too, "but we both know that's not so."

"Maybe it's a work in progress," she admitted. "But it's happening."

"Then what about children?" he asked in the same quiet tone. He smiled slightly—sadly—

when she winced in surprise. "Why do you flinch away in horror whenever the topic arises? You will not even have the conversation, Kiara. Why do you think that is?"

She could see that he knew why it was. But so did she.

And she was no longer afraid.

"Yes," she said, very distinctly. "The very idea of a baby made me feel trapped—choked. Look what happened to my mother! If she hadn't had me, she could have done anything." She reached over then and put her hands on his chest. She felt him stiffen, but he didn't step away. "But I'm letting go of that, Azrin. I'm not my mother. *You* have to trust *me.*"

"Kiara—" But he cut himself off, as if he didn't know what to say for once, and Kiara felt compassion flood through her. His father was dying. He was not only a son coming to terms with his new role in his family, but a king coming to terms with what this must mean for his country. It was not so surprising that he'd done this, when she thought about it that way.

"It's all right," she told him, letting her hands stroke him. Soothing him. Calming him. As she knew only she ever did. Or could. "You don't have to be the king for me, Azrin. You can panic. We're both safe here."

A great shudder worked through his big body, and his eyes closed for a moment. But he opened them again almost at once, and reached down to hold her hands in his—less in a romantic way than to keep her from caressing him, she understood. She didn't protest it.

"What do you want?" he asked, his voice a dark thread of sound. "It never even occurred to me to set you free until now, Kiara. It may never occur to me again. You already know you hate this life. Be very clear about what you want from this."

From me, his dark gaze added. *From any of this*, she thought.

But she knew.

"I'm going to be a terrible queen," she told him, holding his gaze. "I will try hard, but fail you in a thousand ways, because I will never be the kind of woman you *should* have married." She shrugged philosophically. "We will have to find the humor in it."

"And what will you do, as my terrible queen?" He moved his thumbs over the backs of her hands, as if he couldn't quite help himself. She bit back a smile. "Aside from embarrassing me at home and abroad with your antics?"

"Maybe I'll buy a hundred wineries," she said, her pulse leaping beneath her skin when his lips twitched. "Maybe I'll start some new kind of business more appropriate for queens." She was intrigued by the considering gleam in his eyes then, but couldn't let herself get sidetracked. "Maybe I'll figure it out as I go along. But the only thing I know I want, have always wanted, is you."

He looked down at her for a beat of her heart, then another. For a terrible moment she thought he would pull away, but then he drew her hands to his chest instead, and held them there.

"You have always had that," he whispered. "I told you. From that very first moment."

"I love you, Azrin," she whispered back, her voice harsh with emotion. With regret and with promise. With everything they'd come through, together. "I don't want to leave you."

"Then if you love me—" he replied in the same tone, an echo of another time, her own words in that awful hotel room. A past she never wanted to revisit "—don't leave me. Ever again."

She lifted herself on her toes and pressed her mouth to his. Making it real. Feeling the way she trembled all over, and sighing as his arms came around her, strong and hard and true.

He kissed her. He kissed her again and again, as if testing out all the angles for the first time, and she tasted him in the same way, as if she could never get enough of him. Knowing she would never get enough of him. He sank his hands in her hair and she wrapped herself around him, desperate. Demanding.

And in his arms again. Finally.

He shrugged out of his jacket, his shirt. Then he took his time peeling her clothes from her body and worshipping every inch of skin he uncovered. They knelt together on the wide, soft rug and lost themselves in each other. Each touch, each taste, a reaffirmation. A vow.

"Being with you isn't disappearing," Kiara whispered, kissing her way across his chest, his belly. "It's finally being found."

"I will never lose you again," he told her, laying her out on the floor and crawling over her, tasting his way to the center of her feminine heat. "Never."

And then he kissed his way into her, and tore her apart.

Kiara slowly came back to earth. Azrin stripped the rest of his clothes off and then stretched out next to her, deliciously naked. It was enough to make her rise up, her languor forgotten as she climbed over him and took the hard length of him inside of her.

So deep. So good.

Azrin whispered love words in Arabic and English as he began to move. Kiara rode him, heat in her eyes and his hands so demanding on her hips, until he threw her over the edge again and followed her there, calling her name.

And she knew that they were both exactly where they belonged.

Azrin found the bar in Sydney's tony Hyde Park neighborhood almost empty.

He pushed in through the heavy glass doors and shook the wet Australian weather from his clothes. He glanced around at the bartender who stood idly by, polishing glasses, and several waiters in a cluster near the kitchens, all of whom respectfully averted their eyes.

He dismissed them, prowling over to the great windows that looked down on Sydney Harbor, gray and rainy this afternoon. He lowered himself into one of the low leather chairs and only then looked at the effortlessly beautiful woman who sat in the other, still gazing out at the view as if she hadn't noticed him at all.

Though he knew better.

"Let me guess," she said, her voice a throaty sort of murmur that teased over him like a caress, like an open flame. "You are a very boring sort of businessman. Sales, no doubt. In town for a tedious conference of one sort or another and thought you'd pop out for a drink."

"It's as if you are psychic."

He let his gaze play over her. She was exquisite. She sat with perfect, if relaxed, posture in the seat next to his. She was elegance and an impossibly pretty face packed into a black dress that nodded toward the conservative yet still managed to emphasize her sleekly athletic figure, and all of it balanced on wicked, wicked shoes. Her hair was twisted into a smooth chignon, and she had accented both her hair and her ears with the hint of pearls. She looked sleek. And edible.

Mine, he thought.

And still she didn't look at him.

"It's a pity you have so little to recommend you," she said as if she was truly saddened. "I'm in from a lovely visit to the Barossa Valley. I need to find someone at least as exciting as the board meeting I just attended."

She recrossed her legs, drawing his attention to the silken length of them, and those dangerous heels. He pictured them wrapped around his hips and smiled.

"I'm afraid I am not at all exciting," he murmured. "I am a very poor salesman, as it happens. Far duller than a board meeting."

"I should tell you that I'm a single woman on the prowl, in the market for no-strings-attached, mind-altering sex." She let out a disappointed sigh. "Clearly you don't fit the bill."

"What if I make you an offer?" he asked, leaning closer. She turned her head to look at him then and they both smiled. Her brown eyes were merry and mischievous.

And that mouth. How he loved her mouth.

"Hello," she said. And then, her tone turning serious, "I'm listening."

"I'm a married man." He tapped his fingers against the arm of his chair and watched the way her eyes tracked his movements. Hungrily. "But if you like that kind of danger, I can promise you acrobatics. A fierce attention to detail. My wife has insatiable demands."

Her smile widened. She propped her elbow on the wide, flat arm of her leather chair, then rested her chin on her hand as she regarded him. He reached over and traced the fine bones of her wrist, then the line of her forearm.

"Do you mean proper gymnastics?" she asked. "Cartwheels and backflips? Or is that more of a metaphor?"

"The choice is yours." His voice was gallant.

"Meaning it *could* be proper gymnastics." She laughed. "Not an offer you're likely to get just anywhere, I'd think."

"I am a king among men."

She smiled in delight. "So you are."

"Come home with me," he said, ignoring the game completely, his fingers wrapping around her hand and tugging it to his mouth to press a kiss against it. "I want to be inside you more than I want my next breath."

"I love you, too," she said, her own breath catching as she spoke. "But they've cleared out this whole restaurant for us. It would be rude to—"

She broke off as he stood abruptly, and laughed as he offered her his hand.

"Or not," she said. Her mouth curved. "It really is good to be king."

"How is your mother?" he asked when she was standing, her heels putting her right at eye level, all of Sydney laid out behind her, wet and cloudy and at her feet.

"We will always rub each other wrong, I think," Kiara said, but then shrugged it away. "She says she may never come back from Iceland, anyway. She loves it there. And we do very well indeed with all the world between us."

Azrin leaned in and kissed her lightly on that decadent mouth of hers, far more appropriately than he wanted to do. But cleared out restaurant or not, there were still people here. It was still not private. And they were still, and ever, the King and Queen of Khatan. She pulled away from him, smiling ruefully, as if she could read his thoughts.

"Have you thought about the job offer?" he asked.

"It turns out I could probably be a much better consultant than I ever was a vice president." Her eyes sparkled as she looked at him. "But I'm an even better queen."

And so she was. She was not traditional, of course, but as Khatan held its first elections and started down the path toward democracy, there was no need for her to be. If she'd wanted to, she could have been as busy as she'd been before, with all the charities that vied for her patronage and all the places that invited her to speak.

They'd both grown so much this past year. His father's death had forced him to take a cold, hard look at a lot of things. And so had Kiara. It was hard for him to think back to that dark period right after he'd taken the throne. It was hard to imagine he'd come so close to losing her.

He started toward the door, his arm around her. That would never happen again, he vowed. Never.

"I think I'm finally ready," she whispered as

they walked, her face shining as she looked at him, as she leaned in close against his shoulder. "To start trying."

"Ready?" he repeated, but then, suddenly, he knew.

He smiled as a new kind if joy shot through him, and laced his fingers into hers. Holding her tight. He wanted to run his hands over her flat belly, to celebrate the babies they would finally make together, but he couldn't do it here. Not while there were still eyes on them.

But there were a thousand ways to love this woman, his Kiara, and touching her was only part of it.

"I will alert the Khatanian media at once," he teased her instead, grinning when her brown eyes gleamed.

"Don't be silly," she said in the same tone, her cheeks flushed with pleasure. "I've assured your entire extended family they'll be the first to know. Preferably over dinner."

Azrin laughed, and then, at last they headed home.

Together.

* * * * *

Mills & Boon® Large Print

October 2012

A SECRET DISGRACE
Penny Jordan

THE DARK SIDE OF DESIRE
Julia James

THE FORBIDDEN FERRARA
Sarah Morgan

THE TRUTH BEHIND HIS TOUCH
Cathy Williams

PLAIN JANE IN THE SPOTLIGHT
Lucy Gordon

BATTLE FOR THE SOLDIER'S HEART
Cara Colter

THE NAVY SEAL'S BRIDE
Soraya Lane

MY GREEK ISLAND FLING
Nina Harrington

ENEMIES AT THE ALTAR
Melanie Milburne

IN THE ITALIAN'S SIGHTS
Helen Brooks

IN DEFIANCE OF DUTY
Caitlin Crews

Mills & Boon® Large Print
November 2012